John, I'm ashamed to tell you what they were calling her, taunting her as she walked!"

I cringed inwardly because I knew what they were calling her. It had been only a few years since high school when we all called her "Raggy Maggie." And I knew how nicknames like that stuck. I tried not to cringe visibly as I shook my head in mock surprise.

"Well," said the preacher, "I don't think I need to tell you that those boys of mine got what-for when they came home that afternoon. They knew they were wrong, and they've agreed to this punishment. But I'm going to let you in on a secret, John. This isn't really a punishment—it's not even half the lesson. Now, I want your solemn promise that you'll stop by the parsonage on the day after Christmas and pay us a visit."

I agreed, but only reluctantly. I knew that facing that situation again would add nothing to my holiday spirit.

As the preacher headed back to his car, he handed me a sealed envelope as he always did. This way I couldn't argue about being overpaid and was forced to accept his idea of a "fair" price.

After he had driven off, I waited a respectful length of time before I took the envelope out of my pocket and opened it. I was amazed to find two $5 bills inside! In those days the grandest, tallest, best tree on the lot might reach the price of $5, but certainly neither of those did, not by a long shot!

I felt guilty taking $10 for those two trees, because that was about $11 more than I felt they were worth, considering the cost of hauling. Somehow I knew that the preacher was trying to say something by it. But it wasn't until later that I could figure out just what.

I went to the preacher's house on December 26, just as I had promised. And I don't mind telling you that by this time I was rather anxious to see what had become of those trees. I think the preacher must have known this, because he strung me along for quite a while before he finally asked if I wouldn't like to step into their library. This was the room where their Christmas tree was always kept.

As I stepped through the doors I stopped dead in my tracks. There before me was the most beautiful Christmas tree that I'd ever seen! Not only was its shape perfect but there wasn't a bare spot on it. In looking back now I'm still quite without words to describe just how magnificent that tree was.

I stood looking at it for a little while, then I turned to the preacher. "Well," I said, "I'm glad to see you finally gave in and got those kids a decent tree. It's the most beautiful one I've ever seen. But where did you get it, and why did you pay that ridiculous price for those scrubs you got from me?"

"You'd better look closer, John," answered the preacher with a twinkle in his eye, "because those are the trees that you sold us!"

I couldn't believe what I was hearing. I stepped up to the tree and peered into its branches. Only when I looked at it closely could I tell that someone had wired the two trees together, weaving the limbs in to each other very carefully and tenderly. Together, they made one perfect tree.

"Of course, there's been a little adjustment," the preacher chuckled.

"But why would you go to all that trouble? Why

didn't you just pick out a good tree to begin with?" I demanded.

"Well, first of all," said the preacher, "I didn't go to any trouble at all. The boys did. I told them that if they wanted a nice tree badly enough, then they'd have to figure out some way to make one—and they did! I'm sorry that I can't take the credit for it, but all I gave those kids were the trees and what it takes to bind them together. You'll notice there isn't a store-bought ornament on that tree. Everything that makes it beautiful is the result of their loving work. They cared enough about this that they were willing to take something worthless and unattractive and give of themselves whatever was needed to change it into something far better. And I do believe that this is the nicest tree that we've ever had!"

As I looked at the tree, I had to ask, "But why? What did those boys learn from having to construct their own tree?"

"John!" he cried. "Don't you understand it yet? This is the other part of the lesson that you thought was 'punishment' for teasing Maggie. Surely you see, John, that this is what Christmas is really all about. When you and I were all ugly and sick with sin, this is how God cared for us—enough to come down and to do whatever was needed that we might be changed. We're *all* scrub trees, John—you, me, Maggie, everybody. But there's not a one of us on God's green earth that doesn't have the potential to be made into something far more beautiful. We could all be $5*

Christmas trees if we'd only let God change us through the loving work of His Son, Jesus Christ. That same love of His that changes us is what binds us together to make of us something far better than we ever could have been. If my boys learned nothing else from this experience, I at least wanted them to learn that there is no person so plain and no situation so ugly that love cannot change!"

If memory serves me correctly, that was the year I became regular in my church attendance, as I've been these last 45 years. As I look back, I believe it was also about that time that the preacher's boys began to settle down and develop some manners. The older boy became a doctor, and the younger one—well, you children know him as Pastor Bob. He took over our church when his dad passed on.

"But Grandpa," asked the 4-year-old, "what about Raggy Maggie? Did she live happily ever after?"

This youngest granddaughter was used to stories in which all the heroes came out well in the end—and she was young enough not to know the ending of this one. But all her older brothers, sisters, and cousins giggled knowingly as I said, "Well now, that's not for me to say. But I think that first batch of cookies should be just about ready, so why don't we go out to the kitchen and ask her . . ."

Dennis Eberhart, freelance writer, auctioneer, and broker, lives in Kent, Ohio.

*$100 in 2002 money.

This Christmas Business

Margaret E. Sangster, Jr.

Thanks to shy Professor Griswold and the work Agnes did for him, she had money enough for presents for the entire family. As for the professor, he had never known what it was like to be part of a family. In appreciation for all he had done for her, Agnes left him a gift. A very formal gift.

At least she thought she had.

The time was two days before Christmas, and Agnes Lane, college senior, was doing her holiday shopping. The university town boasted only one department store, but that did not bother Agnes, for the store was a well-equipped, charming one, and she was finding plenty of scope for her imagination and her purse. Back home she had a loving, not too small family, so that besides handkerchiefs, ties, and other trifles for teachers and classmates, there were dearer, more personal gifts to be bought. She would give perfume to her mother, who felt that she could never afford really good perfume for herself. A lacy slip would delight Faith, her younger sister, while hockey skates seemed the gift for 13-year-old Louis. There

were those books on art that Richard, her older brother, studying to be an illustrator, so longed to have. Agnes bought all of these gifts very happily, not forgetting a luxurious silk muffler for her father.

She bought happily because she had plenty of money to spend this year, and she could revel in being really extravagant. She had been working all fall, helping the young professor of English with some of his less advanced students.

"You've saved me a lot of worry this term, Miss Lane," the English professor had told her seriously that very afternoon. "I couldn't possibly have been able to give out-of-class instruction to all the ones who needed it."

Agnes had laughed. "I've saved you a lot of trouble perhaps," she told the professor, "but I've also saved considerable of something else for myself! I've put away every cent of money I earned, and I'm going to spend it just as lavishly as possible for Christmas."

The young English professor raised his eyebrows in surprise. Agnes was decidedly aware of the surprise. "Do you know," he said, "I've never been in the least excited about this Christmas business. I never had a mother or a father to fill stockings and trim trees for me. My parents died when I was very small, and I was brought up by a maiden aunt who didn't believe in such silliness."

Agnes sprang to the defense of her favorite holiday. "Christmas isn't in the least silly," she told the professor. "It's grand and splendid and special! I love everything about Christmas. Do you mean to say you don't even like to go Christmas shopping?"

The young professor looked oddly at Agnes. "I haven't any close relatives," he said, "for whom I would buy presents, and I haven't any close friends, either. I've worked pretty hard all my life and—" He paused.

"And you haven't had time to play," Agnes finished for him. "Oh, you're making a great mistake, Mr. Griswold. There's a time in every life for both work and play. This is my fourth year at college, and I think my play times have been almost equally divided with my work times. Surely you will admit that I haven't suffered for it scholastically!"

The young professor sighed. "No, you haven't, Miss Lane," he said. "You're the pupil, to put it ungrammatically, that I'm proudest of. I—" He started to speak and caught himself. "I wish I were like you," he finished lamely.

Agnes did not know what to say, so she didn't say anything; but she smiled kindly on the serious young professor. She didn't know that the impersonal warmth of that smile hurt him more than the lack of it would have done.

* * *

Agnes was a popular person. Her room telephone was always ringing. That was why, when she came home from her Christmas shopping expedition, she had barely time to toss her packages on the bed before things began to happen. It was one of her classmates who telephoned this time. A group of them were getting up a sledding party.

"It'll be the last one before Christmas vacation starts; we'll all be scattering tomorrow," Marcia Hess told her. "You must come along, Aggie. We can't do without you."

Agnes hesitated, but only for a second. "My work's all in order," she said, "so that's all right. But I've just finished buying my Christmas presents, and I wanted to wrap them up at once. I'm going home for Christmas, you

know, and it's a day's trip away. I'll get there at the very last minute, and we always open our gifts on Christmas Eve. I want to be able to open my suitcase and tumble out everything, all ready in its beautiful tissue and silver ribbon. My family," Agnes chuckled, "haven't any idea that I'm going to be so magnificent in the matter of their gifts. They don't know that I've been earning extra money helping Professor Griswold."

"Some people have all the luck," said the girl at the other end of the wire. "Professor Griswold's the handsomest man, even if he is such a sobersides. Imagine being paid to help him!"

Agnes laughed. "He's so serious," she said, "that I scarcely ever think of him as being handsome! Well," she was weakening, "I can't desert you, and that's the truth. I'll wrap my presents in a hurry and put the cards on them and meet you wherever you say. After all, I'm in the mood for a party!"

The presents were not hard to wrap, and Agnes Lane had bought such lovely paper to wrap them in! Her presents were going to take the prize for good looks—on the outside, at least. She wrapped them carefully, and as she came to the last one of all, she smiled. The last present was a set of handsome bookends—and it was a present she would not take home.

"I'll give the professor a thrill," Agnes chuckled to herself as she wrapped the bookends in the cheeriest of the paper. "Christmas is silly, is it? Oh, I'll send him a present, and he'll like it!"

The bookends were certainly attractive. They were slim and long and were carved from some sort of sandstone. They were as cold and impersonal a gift, however, as the stone from which they were fashioned. *It's best to be impersonal with one's professor*, thought Agnes, as she fixed the last bow in place and wrote on the card: "With best wishes from your pupil and helper."

She set that gift a little aside from the others which were to go into her suitcase. Then with the consciousness of a task finished and a good time ahead, she slipped into a rosy turtleneck sweater and a little matching rose-colored beret and went out to meet the classmates who were waiting for her. During an evening filled with merriment, bonfires, songs, and toasted marshmallows, Agnes quite forgot about the young professor who had never had much fun, whose life had been a serious matter because his parents had died when he was a baby, and he had been brought up by a stern aunt.

* * *

Agnes reached home late from the sleigh ride. She was so drowsy from the exercise and the cold air that she was glad indeed she had not left her presents to be wrapped at the last second. Sleepily, she tumbled them from the bed into a suitcase. Some of the cards fell off in the process, but she attached them again to their proper bundles.

The presents that were to be delivered in the college town she put casually into a separate pile. The handyman of the dormitory would deliver them for her in the morning. She had already given him his instructions.

With a word of fervent prayer that reflected the joyous spirit of Christmas, she tumbled into her bed to enjoy the sleep of youth and good health until morning. With morning came the final hurry and rush, the business of scrambling into clothes, fastening bags together, and dashing for the train that would take her home. It was, as she had explained, an all-day ride to her hometown. She would arrive there late in the evening, just in time for the lighting of the Christmas tree and the opening of the gifts, for this was Christmas Eve.

As she boarded the train and settled back comfortably against the cushions, Agnes told herself, with a sigh, that she would have a needed period of quiet before meeting with her dear ones. Yet as she sat in the train she was oddly enough not thinking of her dear ones. For some strange reason she was thinking instead of the young professor whom she had helped with his work during the months past. Suddenly she saw him as a sad, tragic, childish figure, a little boy who had never played enough! She wished that she had bought him something a little more frivolous than bookends—some colorful neckties, perhaps, or some embroidered handkerchiefs. All at once, then, she was putting the thoughts sternly aside; for the young professor was attractive to her, even though she had almost denied it to her friend, and she would not want him to know how she felt about him.

* * *

Agnes Lane reached home when the late winter dusk was falling. The whole family was waiting at the station to meet her, except Mother. Mother was at home, keeping the dinner hot. Agnes was completely surrounded by a babble of excited tongues. Her father tucked her into the car beside him; her two brothers, the older and the younger, and her sister, piled into the rear seat. Over her shoulder Agnes called back her big news.

"I've got presents for you, grand presents," she exulted. "I know you didn't think I'd bring anything home except maybe a cake or a box of fudge or something, but I've been a wage earner this year. And I've spent practically all my booty on you folk."

The young sister's eyes grew round, and the older brother said, "You're a wonderful sis." And the younger brother asked, "Oh, boy, what did you bring me?"

They were then piling out of the car at the home door, and Agnes' mother was standing in the doorway with her arms outflung. Agnes, after she had received the loving kiss and given a smothering one in return, rushed into the parlor where the Christmas tree stood. "Watch! I'm going to open my suitcase right in front of the tree," she cried.

Her mother was laughing. "Extravagant child," she said. "But we'll love our gifts, all the same, and we hope you'll love the ones we have for you. Directly after dinner we'll open everything."

Directly after dinner, they did. Mother came first. What she thought of the perfume could only be measured by the ecstatic sparkle in her eyes, while the younger sister was so delighted over the pretty underwear that she could not speak. As for the older brother, he retired into a corner immediately with his books.

It was the younger brother, however, whose face reflected the greatest amazement when he untied the brilliant wrappings that shrouded his package. "My land, Sis!" he exclaimed. "What are they?"

Agnes, absorbed in opening her own presents, looked up and saw with startled eyes that Louis was holding a slim sandstone object in each hand. For one sickening moment she remembered how some of the cards had come dislodged, and how she had replaced them. She was then laughing hysterically and wondering what Professor Griswold would do with the skates she had unwittingly sent him.

"Oh, brother," she explained, "I've made the silliest error! I bought you beautiful hockey skates and these"— she was fairly rocking with her mirth—"these are the bookends I bought for my English professor. I must have mixed the packages. But don't you worry—you'll get your skates. I'll even get you some in town day after tomorrow, if necessary. You won't have to wait until I get back to college."

The youngster's eyes were bright. "I wanted skates something awful. I couldn't guess what these were!" He indicated the bookends. "I kinda thought," he chuckled, "that you'd gone crazy."

Agnes was still laughing, but her laughter was not gay anymore. She was picturing Professor Griswold's blank amazement and shock when he opened the frivolous, childish pair of hockey skates.

* * *

When Agnes returned to her dormitory room at the end of the Christmas vacation, she was amazed to find that room a bower of roses. The housekeeper met her at the door with a twinkle in her eyes. "A gentleman brought the flowers," she said, "but you'll never guess who!"

"No, I won't," said Agnes. "Tell me!"

The housekeeper smiled. "It was Professor Griswold," she said. She smiled broadly. "He is waiting in the parlor to see you now."

Agnes went into the parlor like a scared, spanked child. Her cheeks were flaming. She had spent a good many hours thinking about this time of explanation. She hesitated on the threshold of the parlor, hesitated and was quite unprepared for the forward rush of the serious young man who came swiftly to meet her. She was even less prepared for the arms that were suddenly around her.

"Oh, my darling," said Professor Griswold's unmistakable voice, but with a new note in it. "I've been so dreadfully in love with you all year, and I never dreamed that you felt the same way about me. I didn't dare hope until your Christmas gift came, such a happy Christmas gift, and such a card with it! I'll"—he had disengaged one arm from the unresisting, bewildered Agnes and was fumbling in his pocket—"I'll never part with this card."

Professor Griswold did not seem to notice that Agnes had, so far, been speechless. "'This is a good time present,'" he quoted from the card that he now held in one hand. "'And it goes to you with all my love. Be a nice boy and enjoy wearing them.'

"Agnes, darling," said the professor shyly, having finished with the card, "I spent this whole Christmas vacation learning to skate."

He stopped talking swiftly. "Why, I haven't—

I haven't kissed you yet!" he said in a startled tone.

Oddly enough, Agnes decided that she was rather looking forward to a new experience. She knew now why the professor had so completely filled her mind. She realized with a start that he had been filling her heart as well.

Margaret E. Sangster, Jr. (1894-1981), was born in Brooklyn, New York. She was an editor, scriptwriter, journalist, short story writer, and novelist. Easily, she was—and remains—one of the most beloved inspirational writers of her age.

In Remembrance of Me

Wilbur Hendricks

It was December 23, 1945, and the troops were cold and lonely as their "Forty-and-Eight" boxcar rumbled through the night. The next day the train stopped at Munich, where they hoped to trade food for candles.

A small 10-year-old boy nervously approached their car.

The dirty "Forty-and-Eight" was to be our home for several days as it rumbled over the railroad tracks of northern Germany. The time: December 23, 1945. We were occupation troops fresh from the States to replace battle-weary GIs, eager to return home now that the war had ended.

Our troopship had docked the day before at Bremerhaven after a rough 11-day crossing on the cold Atlantic. Two weeks before we had mingled with happy, carefree Christmas shoppers in New York City. It was the first peacetime Christmas for our nation in four years.

Today in our "Forty-and-Eight" boxcar (a name carried over from World War I for the German boxcars that held 40 men or eight mules) we were lonesome, homesick, torn apart from families and friends.

The night of December 23 was a nightmare. In the darkness we were tossed from end to end of the boxcar as it stopped and started. There were a few straw ticks provided for us if we cared to try to catch some sleep. But such attempts were useless, as those who were still standing or moving about fell over our forms on the floor in the darkness of the boxcar.

At noon on the twenty-fourth, as we sat on the floor in groups eating from the box rations that had been provided for us, one of the fellows hit upon a great idea. We passed around a transparent bag, and each of us put one item of food from our rations into the bag. We hoped that the next time the train stopped for a while we might trade the food for some candles.

One of the fellows in our group spoke German, so we asked him to negotiate for us. Our train went on and on through the German countryside. Nighttime came and still we were going. We had just about given up hope when we pulled into the large railroad yards at Munich and stopped.

Our friend immediately began calling out into the darkness. Soon a small frail boy of about 10 slowly approached our car. We could imagine his fear as just a few months before we had been his country's enemy. He was baffled that one of us knew his language so well, and what did we want of him? One of the men struck a match and the bag glistened beautifully. Our spokesman explained to the boy that the bag of food would be his if he could get some candles to us before we left. His mouth gaped open, his eyes stared at the bag for a moment, then he dashed off into the darkness. We didn't realize then that there probably was more food in that bag than he had ever seen at one time.

With each creak and groan of our car we felt sure our train was leaving. But after what seemed an eternity we could see the boy's form coming back toward us, sometimes almost falling over the tracks as he ran.

One of the fellows lit a match as the boy reached the side of our car. He set a brown bag on the floor. In it were eight homemade candles in cupcake papers. We immediately lit one, and it cast a feeble but warm glow in our boxcar. We decided not to light more than one at a time in hopes that the eight might last the entire night. We thanked the boy and gave him the food. He then pulled his other hand from behind his back. In it he held a branch from a Christmas tree, about 18 inches long. On it was a single strand of tinsel. We set it in the crack in the floor. The tinsel sparkled in the crisp breeze and reflected the glow of our flickering candle.

Then we heard sounds that told us our train was on its way. We shouted thanks to the boy as he stood and waved goodbye to us.

A deep silence fell over our group, and slowly we gathered into a circle around our candle and "tree." Some in front sat cross-legged on the floor. Others knelt behind them, and the third row stood. I don't recall just who really began, but we took turns at our Christmas Eve worship service. We didn't have enough light to read our pocket-size New Testaments, but we recited some Scriptures the best we could from memory. We sang Christmas carols, there were sentence prayers, and one of the fellows gave a short impromptu meditation.

And then we had communion. We had no bread or wine, but we spoke the words—"Take, eat: this is my body, which is broken for you"—and we touched our lips. Then—"This cup is the new testament in my blood: this do ye, as oft as ye drink it, in remembrance of me." Again we touched our lips. Softly we sang "Silent Night," then spoke a benediction.

Slowly the circle broke up. Our loneliness and homesickness seemed to be gone. We felt a great friendship toward one another. We knew we had just been given the greatest gift we had ever received.

* * *

Many Christmases have come and gone, and I've attended communion almost every Christmas Eve. The services have been beautiful with tall lighted tapers, silver service, plush carpeting—everything to make a beautiful experience. These services have meant a lot to me, but my thoughts still go back many years to a dirty boxcar, a circle of lonely GIs, a homemade candle in a cupcake paper, a tree branch with a lone strand of tinsel, a frail German boy, and the solemn words *Do this in remembrance of me.*

Wilbur Hendricks wrote for popular magazines during the second half of the twentieth century.

Lipstick Like Lindsay's

Gerald R. Toner

In the name of Saint Nicholas and his God he had glibly promised his little daughter Jennie that for Christmas she would indeed have "crayon lipstick like Lindsay Schell's." What a simple request. And cheap! Piece of cake. Plenty of time to pick one up later.

Then a week before Christmas, in drizzling rain, he entered Children's Palace and asked for the crayon lipstick. It wasn't there! So he went to drugstore after drugstore, in town after town, city after city. Nowhere was there so much as one tube of "lipstick like Lindsay's."

He finally reached the end and knew himself to be an utter failure as a father. By then it was December 23, and with a sense of utter futility he faced the ordeal of delivering the heartbreaking news to Jennie.

In the fourth century, when the tales and memory of Christ were still young, there lived a man named Nicholas, who was bishop of the city of Myra in Lycia, Asia Minor. History has it that he was persecuted and martyred by Emperor Diocletian. Thereafter, he became the patron saint of children, remembered for the gifts he left in secret in memory of Christ's birth. While much about his life is legend, his custom of giving gifts is a fact, and it is a custom that has without fail been entrusted to willing disciples throughout the centuries.

Under such a discipleship and acting under Saint Nicholas's guidance, I hoisted my daughter to my knee and inquired as to her secret list for Christmas. I take this assignment from Saint Nicholas seriously. I always have.

Jennie spoke directly to the point. "I want crayon lipstick like Lindsay Schell's."

"What else would you like?"

Jennie thought long and hard. She was only 4 years old and had not learned the words "BMW" or "mink." In fact, it became very clear that she had thought carefully in anticipation of this moment of list making, and the "crayon lipstick like Lindsay Schell's" was not only paramount, it was exclusive. I suggested a few odds and ends, and we sealed the letter to Saint Nicholas with love and kisses.

Jennie's discovery of the crayon lipstick in question had been fortuitous. She knew about real lipstick, of course, and about play lipstick that was barely visible to the naked eye and totally innocuous to the keeper of a child's clothes. But this was a look-like-a-crayon-deep-colored-apparently-harmless-and-supposedly-hypo-allergenic stick of chemicals that spread like real lipstick. Lindsay, age 6 and more worldly wise than Jennie, had come to the house one night for pizza with her mother and father and shared her lipstick with Jennie. From that point on it became a fixed object on Jennie's wish list.

I was, at first, amused and delighted. God's miracles

come, on occasion, in small packages, and I knew that one day Jennie might develop a similar fervor for more expensive gifts. Thus, for this year, Jennie's wishes and Santa Claus's orders to myself were commensurate with my budgetary constraints. The crayon lipstick could not possibly cost more than $2.50. In short, an easy task had been laid out for Saint Nicholas and, therefore, myself as his agent.

My wife urged me not to delay. She was wise, and I was not. A few weeks passed. The memory of Thanksgiving faded into December and Christmas preparations. Work at the office took on a double-time cadence as every attorney in town tried to pack the month of December into its first two weeks, knowing that the only thing that would be packed in the last two weeks would be the bags of every attorney in town. It was the fifteenth of the month before I began to catch up with the joy of the season.

We bought our tree, and Jennie spoke about "crayon lipstick like Lindsay Schell's." We finished our Christmas cards and began reading our favorite Christmas stories, and Jennie giggled in anxious anticipation of a "crayon lipstick like Lindsay Schell's." We lit our Advent candles, and I could tell that she was dreaming not of sugar plums but of crayon lipstick. I smiled, knowing that Saint Nicholas would allow me to fulfill her desire at any of a dozen drugstores, department stores, and even supermarkets within two miles of our home.

And then one early evening after a medical deposition in the vicinity of numerous shopping centers, I decided to make a quick trip to the local Children's Palace and swiftly accomplish my assignment. Through most of the year the roads that lead through the chaos of shopping center land are merely an endless array of erratic lights and signs. At Christmas time they become a snarling mass of harried Christmas shoppers. Inching my way through the traffic to the correct curb cut for Children's Palace, I turned in just as a steady downpour erased all possible visibility through my windshield.

It rained from then on, all the way to Christmas. That is not literary license. It just happened that way. It rained and didn't seem to stop. If it did stop it was while I was asleep or in the office. If I made the slightest move for the door or got into my car to drive anywhere, it would start raining.

I found the only parking place available, having hovered about the lot for what seemed a modest eternity. Typical fortune found me about 10 yards from the expressway and 60 yards from the front door of the store without an umbrella. I sighed, "Such are the wages of virtue," rolled up my pants a turn or two, thrust open my door, and puddle jumped to the entrance of the toy store.

Inside the store, with a light steam rising off my suit, I began wandering up and down the aisles in search of either the play makeup or an employee. Since all employees in discount stores are either on break or disguised as customers, I found the play makeup first. They had Tinkerbell, Bo-Po, Barbie, and numerous other concoctions, but no crayon lipstick.

After a modicum of stealth, I trapped an unsuspecting employee and asked her for the crayon lipstick. I carefully described the object of my search and slowly, as "through a glass, darkly," she showed a glimmer of recognition.

"Yeah. We had that."

"Great," I replied, trying to ignore her use of the past tense. "Where is it?"

No one in this position ever gives a completely straight answer. She responded, "It was on aisle 13."

"I looked on aisle 13, and it's not there," I began, "but maybe if you'll come with me, we'll find it. I probably just didn't see it." I have learned that a plea of stupidity will often work wonders in such instances. She smiled and nodded, and we walked together to aisle 13.

"It used to be there," she said. "But we must have sold out."

"Could you check for me?" I asked.

"Hey, Margie," she called out. An older woman emerged from a wall of boxed big wheels, where she had been hiding. "This man wants to know if we got any play lipsticks."

Before I could interrupt, Margie had educated me as to the various other lipsticks that could be found on aisle 13. I then noted politely that I was searching for a specific crayon lipstick like Santa Claus had brought Lindsay the year before. She noted that Jennie would not know the difference. I assured her that Jennie would.

"Well, we had them. But they sold out. I don't know if we'll be getting any more in before Christmas, or not."

There was really nothing more to say. I thanked them, and thinking to myself that I had just dried out, I went back into the rain. "This might be a little harder than I thought," I told myself as I hugged the wall of the building in a futile attempt to avoid the downpour, and went around the corner to Service Merchandise.

I was no more fortunate in the home of catalogue sales. "I remember those. They looked like crayons. Real

popular a while back."

"Right," I said eagerly.

"We don't have 'em."

"Gonna get 'em back?"

"I couldn't say. You never can tell."

I went on to the Walgreen's drugstore next door. "Crayon lipstick?"

I believe the woman thought I was a little odd.

"It's for Christmas . . . my little girl," I said.

"Try aisle five."

I tried aisle five and found only real lipstick. Evidently, she hadn't believed my story about Christmas and my little girl. I checked aisle seven for toys and found only the usual collection of non-crayon and, therefore, inferior children's play makeup.

I made my way back to the car, got in, and turned on the radio only to have the newscaster remind me that it was December 17, "just seven shopping days left before Christmas." I pulled the car back into what is euphemistically referred to as the "flow of traffic" but which was, at the moment, actually more like a trickle or a drip, and worked my way down the strip.

An inconsequential errand, casually made on the heels of a deposition, had not gone at all as expected. Rather than leave well enough alone for the time being, I stopped at Thornbury's, the oldest toy store on the strip, knowing that I would pay a lot more, but confident that I would find what I wanted. While a young sales clerk was far more interested in my request, she had even less help to offer. She knew what I wanted, but they hadn't stocked the item for weeks—maybe months.

The word "months" sent a sudden chill through me.

What if I had run into not just a streak of bad luck but an outright famine? I walked away from Thornbury's Toys with growing concern. They hadn't even suggested a place I might purchase a tube of crayon lipstick.

I glanced at my watch and noticed it was almost 7:00. Already late for dinner, I headed down the road for home, determined that the next day would bring better luck. Then, like a gambler drawn to that one last slot machine, prime for the plucking, I noticed the Woolworth's sign over to my right. *Well, why not?* I asked myself, signaling quickly and pulling into a space.

The store was everything a dime store should be. Musty, dusty, and old, it was the type of place that still sold rubber spoolies for women's hair. It was perfect for my purposes. I went straight to the manager.

"Do you have—or have you carried—a type of play lipstick that looks like a crayon?"

"Sure," he said.

Here was a man's man. A giant among men. A hero from his clip-on tie down to the pointed ends of his shoes.

"They're right back here." And he personally led me to a pegboard at the back of the store.

Our eyes searched the pegboard together. There was an ominous metal hook that was empty. He didn't have to tell me, but he did anyway.

"They were right there."

"But you sold out the last one a week or so ago," I offered.

"That's right." He smiled. "But the other stores might have some left."

"Could you check?"

"I'll be glad to," he said. And with that, he initiated a series of phone calls, during which I found that Woolworth's was closing its stores in the area. All of their stock had, in fact, been moved to Lexington. But they did remember the crayon lipstick.

"I'm awful sorry I couldn't help," he said. I knew that he was sincere and thanked him for his help and his sincerity. My way home was filled with a grim determination shadowed by slowly increasing panic.

When I laid the situation out to my wife, she stated that which I already knew: "You started too late, sweetheart."

"You are right," I said with a certain amount of hurt pride. "But do you have any ideas?"

"Keep trying drugstores and dime stores."

"I will," I said. "I will," I mumbled to myself.

And the next day I began the phone calls. I started with the remaining toy and discount stores. An entire morning of otherwise billable hours was spent in large part "on hold" while the search for the elusive lipstick was made. I have no idea whether they all searched their counters and shelves or stood around waiting for the light on the phone to go out so they could go back on break. But I never hung up. And finally a pleasant enough woman at a Target department store acknowledged my request, telling me she was familiar with the product, and that she had it in the store.

My excitement knew no bounds. I made my excuses at the office and slipped away during lunch. The store was a good 15 minutes away by car, and under normal circumstances I would never have made the trip. But now, of course, these were not normal circumstances. And I was glad to give up lunch if I met with success.

31

I didn't. I searched the Target store and found neither lipstick nor helpful employees. My informant had been ill-informed, and I had been led astray. I ate a Hershey bar for lunch as I drove back to the office.

On Thursday night Jennie and I were in the kitchen making cookies when the phone rang. I answered. I could tell it was long distance. "May I speak with a little girl named Jennie?"

I knew immediately it was the boss himself, the man in charge—in two words, Santa Claus. I gave the phone to Jennie.

"Hello? Yes, this is Jennie." There was a pause, then a giggle of delight. She cupped her little hand over the receiver. "It's Santa Claus, Daddy," she whispered.

"I know," I whispered back. For the previous two years my special contacts with Saint Nicholas had prompted this annual phone call. It was made from a friend's house in Cincinnati, 100 miles away. I kept stirring the oats into the batter as I listened to her conversation.

"Yes, I've been a good girl . . ."

Another pause while I held my breath.

"I want a crayon lipstick, just like Lindsay Schell's."

My heart sank. The conversation had quickly taken on the tenor of a conspiracy. If ever I have wished that the cup would be passed on to a more worthy agent of Saint Nicholas, it was at that moment. Jennie ended her conversation, aglow with the magic of Christmas.

The next morning I took desperate measures. First, I called Carol Schell, Lindsay's mother. I explained my dilemma. "Carol, could you look at Lindsay's lipstick and give me the name of the manufacturer?"

"Of course," she said, immediately responding to the shrill edge of abject fear in my voice. "But I'll have to find it first."

"I'll wait," I replied. And I waited until Carol returned to the phone several minutes later.

"Are you still there?"

"Where else?" I laughed, ignoring the mounting stack of return phone call slips that my secretary was dutifully placing before me.

"I've got it. Have you got a pencil and paper?"

"You bet," I responded, and meticulously repeated and copied the information.

When I had thanked Carol and hung up, my secretary came in and stood at the end of my desk. She looked at me and smiled warmly.

"I overheard what you were doing. You are a very special daddy."

"If I were really a special daddy," I said, "I wouldn't be in this fix now."

"Hmmm," she said, and handed me a piece of paper with the Manhattan area code written on it.

I got the number and tried to remain calm as the receptionist answered.

"Hi, my name is— Well, you don't care about that, but you see, I'm a lawyer . . . and . . ."

"You want the legal department?" she interrupted.

"No, no I want, uh, your consumer ombudsman."

"Just a moment," she responded. I was momentarily impressed with my ability to move right to the source of all knowledge. That apparent skill, however, was soon outdistanced by my persistence. Three more departments and 10 minutes later I finally stumbled onto the

CHRISTMAS
IN MY HEART

11

JOE L. WHEELER

REVIEW AND HERALD® PUBLISHING ASSOCIATION
HAGERSTOWN, MD 21740

This book was
Edited by Jeannette R. Johnson
Designed by Tina M. Ivany
Electronic makeup by Toya M. Koch
Cover illustration by Superstock/Currier & Ives
Interior illustrations from the library of Joe L. Wheeler
Typeset: 11/12 Goudy

PRINTED IN U.S.A.

06 05 04 03 02   5 4 3 2

R&H Cataloging Service
Wheeler, Joe L., 1936-   comp.
    Christmas in my heart. Book 11.

    1. Christmas stories, American.   I. Title:
Christmas in my heart. Book 11.

ISBN 0-8280-1717-4

Dedication

As we look back through the years at those people who have done the most to keep *Christmas in My Heart* and other story anthologies going, a number of story-submitters come immediately to mind. Some have lent us their entire collection, others have given us these collections (the labor of a lifetime to accumulate), declaring that no one else they know could possibly need them or value them more than we. Some send us their favorite stories, and we never hear from them again.

Yet others, a precious Gideon's band, are always on the prowl for stories they feel would meet our needs. Of them all, however, one person stands out, for she chooses only winners, those stories that are powerful enough, moving enough, to compete with the best. She types out most of these for us and seeks to find their origins before mailing us another batch. Year after year passes, and still she searches.

It is time we honor this indefatigable contributor. It gives me great joy to dedicate *Christmas in My Heart 11* to this most faithful of our story submitters:

MARILYN NELSON

of

College Place, Washington

Books by Joe L. Wheeler

Christmas in My Heart, books 1-11
Christmas in My Heart, audio books 1-6
Easter in My Heart
Everyday Heroes
Great Stories Remembered, I
Great Stories Remembered, II
Great Stories Remembered, III
Great Stories Remembered, audio books I-III
Great Stories Remembered Classic Books (12 books)
Heart to Heart Stories of Dads
Heart to Heart Stories of Moms
Heart to Heart Stories of Friendship
Heart to Heart Stories of Love
Heart to Heart Stories of Sisters
Old-time Christmas Stories
Remote Controlled
Stories of Angels
The Twelve Stories of Christmas
Time for a Story
View at Your Own Risk
What's So Good About Tough Times?
Wings of God, The

To order, call 1-800-765-6955.
Visit us at www.reviewandherald.com for information on other Review and Herald products.

Acknowledgments

"Serenity at Christmas" (Introduction), by Joseph Leininger Wheeler, Copyright 2002. Printed by permission of the author.

"And the Two Were Made One," by Dennis Eberhart. Printed by permission of the author.

"This Christmas Business," by Margaret E. Sangster, Jr. Published in December 24, 1932, *Young People's Weekly*. Reprinted by permission of Joe Wheeler (P.O. Box 1246, Conifer, CO 80433) and David C. Cook Ministries, Colorado Springs, Colorado.

"In Remembrance of Me," by Wilbur Hendricks. Published in December 1970 *Sunshine Magazine*. Reprinted by permission of Garth Henrichs, publisher of Sunshine Publications. If anyone can provide knowledge of where the author (or author's next of kin) can be found, please send to Joe Wheeler (P.O. Box 1246, Conifer, CO 80433).

"Lipstick Like Lindsay's," by Gerald R. Toner. Published in *Lipstick Like Lindsay's and Other Christmas Stories*. Reprinted by permission of the publisher, Pelican Publishing Company, Inc., and the author.

"At Lowest Ebb," author unknown. If anyone can provide knowledge of the authorship and earliest publication of this old story, please send that information to Joe Wheeler (P.O. Box 1246, Conifer, CO 80433).

"Christmas Love," by Ellen Austin. Published in December 1983 *Sunshine Magazine*. Reprinted by permission of Garth Henrichs, publisher of Sunshine Publications. If anyone can provide knowledge of where the author (or author's next of kin) can be found, please send to Joe Wheeler (P.O. Box 1246, Conifer, CO 80433).

"The Christmas Doll," author unknown. If anyone can provide knowledge of the authorship and earliest publication of this old story, please send that information to Joe Wheeler (P.O. Box 1246, Conifer, CO 80433).

"You Are Never Too Old," by Myrtle Edna Rouse. If anyone can provide knowledge of the authorship and earliest publication of this old story, please send that information to Joe Wheeler (P.O. Box 1246, Conifer, CO 80433).

"Two Red Apples," author unknown. Published in *Your Story Hour*, vol. 1. Reprinted by permission of Joe Wheeler (P.O. Box 1246, Conifer, CO 80433), Your Story Hour (an interfaith independent ministry), and Review and Herald® Publishing Association.

"Angela's Christmas," by Julia Schayer. Published

in *A Budget of Christmas Tales*, by Charles Dickens and others (Bible House, New York: Christian Herald, 1895). Text used by permission of Christian Herald Ministries.

"The Best Christmas Pageant Ever," by Barbara Robinson. Published in December 1967 *McCall's*; republished in December 1982 issue. Also published in December 1986 *Focus on the Family Magazine*. Reprinted by permission of the author.

"One to Cherish," by Lucy Parr. Published in December 1974 *Sunshine Magazine*. Reprinted by permission of Garth Henrichs, publisher of Sunshine Publications. If anyone can provide knowledge of where the author (or author's next of kin) can be found, please send to Joe Wheeler (P.O. Box 1246, Conifer, CO 80433).

"The Easter Christmas Tree," by Arlene Anibal (as told to Marilyn Tworog). Published in December 18, 1979, *Lake Union Herald*. Reprinted by permission of *Lake Union Herald*. If anyone can provide knowledge of where the author (or author's next of kin) can be found, please send to Joe Wheeler (P.O. Box 1246, Conifer, CO 80433).

"The Christmas Stocking," by Julie Rae Rickard. Published in December 1999 *The War Cry*. Reprinted by permission of Salvation Army's *The War Cry*, and the author.

"The Ragged Red Coat," by Karen A. Williams. Published in November/December 1982 *Virtue Magazine*. If anyone can provide knowledge of where the author (or author's next of kin) can be found, please send to Joe Wheeler (P.O. Box 1246, Conifer, CO 80433).

"Evensong," by Joseph Leininger Wheeler. Originally published in Wheeler's *The Twelve Stories of Christmas* (Tulsa, Oklahoma: RiverOaks Publishing, 2001). Reprinted by permission of the author.

Contents

Snowed In

If I could have but one gift this Christmas
    It would be this:
    To be snowed in with all the power lines down
        Snowed in with all the roads closed
        Snowed in with a telephone that cannot ring
        Snowed in with a computer that cannot work.

    To be snowed in with you
        Snowed in with those I love most
        Snowed in with cord after cord of seasoned firewood
        Snowed in with kerosene lanterns

Snowed in with an old woodstove
Snowed in with stacks of handmade quilts
Snowed in with music to sing and perform
Snowed in with parlor games to play
Snowed in with books to read and stories to tell
Snowed in with pantry shelves groaning under the weight of food.
Snowed in with the Lord's sweet, sweet spirit
Snowed in with Christmas.

That is all I ask:
    To be snowed in.

—Joseph Leininger Wheeler

Serenity at Christmas

Joseph Leininger Wheeler

Serenity at Christmas? Surely you jest! Why, thanks to nonstop shopping and wrapping of gifts, getting off the annual batch of Christmas cards (each with its personalized note), getting ready for the annual invasion of Christmas guests, attending all the school programs the kids are involved with, helping out in the church's Christmas activities—oh! And not incidentally, keeping up with the constant demands of career, marriage, and family . . . You must be losing it. Serenity indeed!

Well, I must admit it sounds a bit farfetched, but serenity is possible. Permit me to explain.

The Christmas season may be every bit as hectic—or as serene—as we make it. We are the determiners. All too often we forget this, acting as if we are prisoners of forces beyond our control. Having said that, however, I must hasten to add this qualifier: never in human history has serenity been more difficult to achieve. What with telephone, cell phone, fax, e-mail, pager, computer, laptop, TV, CD-Rom, DVD, cinema, radio, videos, books, magazines, newspapers, catalogues (plus, the church, career, filial, marital, and familial worlds),

not to forget the 50,000 commercials to which each of us is exposed during a given calendar year—well, where in all this is serenity to be found?

Let's find out.

First of all, we must each define the parameters of our Christmas season. If we think for a moment that we are going to cram all the cacophony, activity, and greed of the year into a day or two, achieving serenity would be a virtual impossibility. For serenity, a longer Christmas season is an absolute essential.

I suggested in my *Christmas in My Heart*, Book 2, introduction, "The 36 Days of Christmas," that all of us ought to begin our Christmas season on Thanksgiving Evening. Clean out the Thanksgiving-related debris, decorate the house for Christmas, put up the crèche and, perhaps, even put up the Christmas tree. Begin the Christmas season that evening, by unplugging almost everything electronic from family life. As for that brazen intruder, the telephone, the important calls can be retrieved from the answering machine later. A fire in the fireplace, candles, kerosene lamps, each will contribute to the desired atmosphere of serenity, as will stories.

But even before all this, discipline is needed. Discipline is an old-fashioned word not much in vogue in today's permissive if-it-feels-good-do-it age, an age that often appears nearly devoid of respect for others, kindness, and empathy. Serenity will be impossible to achieve in households where parents have abdicated control and handed it over to their children.

Changes are in the wind, however. More and more often I am seeing parents courageous enough to regain control of the avenues to their children's minds, hearts,

9

and souls. These parents say, in effect, that God did not entrust this responsibility to the talking heads on television or to the advertisers who are in our face every moment of the day; not even to school administrators and teachers, or church administrators or preachers. But God *did* entrust that responsibility to each father and each mother, the ultimate guardians of the children they bear. Even the law agrees: When school administrators and teachers exercise control over children, the legal term for it is *in loco parentis* (acting in the parental role in the absence of the parents).

Today such parents are reassuming responsibilities their own parents may have surrendered by default. They are willing to be tough in their loving, to recognize that while an ideal home ought to be run by democratic rules that are fair, there must be a court of final resort—someone must be willing to make final decisions when there is no achievable consensus.

Thus, as a given family enters that first day of the Christmas season, wise parents welcome it with positiveness, enthusiasm, and joy. They don't ask for a vote: "Shall we observe Christmas reverentially this year?" Instead, they operate as though they have an understood consensus: "Tonight begins our Christmas story season. You'll remember that some of the stories we share are new ones, while others are stories you already love. Tonight we'll vote. Which will it be: an old one—or a new one?"

And it will go on from there: "This Christmas, wouldn't it be special to make our gifts personal, instead of just things we buy?" Discuss ways gifts could be made and ask for personal preferences so children don't end up making the same things. Ask for family input in terms of how to make this Christmas a more meaningful one. Attend Christmas plays, concerts, oratorios. Help those who are in need. Pay particular attention to lonely and unvisited senior citizens. Mentor a child who is neglected by others. Invite friends to join the family on game nights. Occasionally take turns helping to bake or prepare Christmas "deliciosities." Do unexpected, fun things. But through it all, let no one forget whose birth and life the season celebrates.

During this Christmas season the family unit is to be a sacred one, and all are expected to participate in the announced activities, because if some do not, the magic of the season will immediately break down. If the television set is turned on, if neighbor children set the agenda for some of the family, if children tune out the family with earphones, if the telephone is allowed to dominate, if computer games are permitted to take over—well, any one of these is capable of destroying this Christmas serenity.

Each day of the Advent is to be celebrated in a special way, each complete with at least one story or reading from a Christmas book. Occasionally, a beloved Christmas film or video will be seen by the entire family. Grandparents, especially, are to be drawn into this circle of activities. And joy should remain paramount if children are to retain their love for the season. It should be a time in which to make memories, a time to assemble the extended family from time to time.

Families may even wish to study Christmas as it is observed around the world, trying out the most interesting traditions to see if they ought to be incorporated in the family's most beloved traditions in future Christmases. Traditions such as Mexico's "Las Posadas" (see "The 36 Days of Christmas," in *Christmas in My Heart,* book 2), or St. Nicholas, as lowland Europe celebrates his coming, beginning in mid-November and ending with the Eve of St. Nicholas on December 5 (see *Christmas in My Heart,* book 6). Christmas music from other countries can be listened to and performed, as well.

At last it will come, Christmas Eve itself. By now the entire family will be in the mood to remember the Christ Child. The presents will have already been made, wrapped, and given away or placed under the tree. The children will have participated earlier in writing Christmas letters or cards. Christmas candy and cookies—ah, their fragrance is everywhere! Family comes. In many homes Christmas presents are opened, and later the Trading Game is played. (See "Hans and the Trading Game," *Christmas in My Heart,* book 5.) At midnight some families may go to church; others will prefer to attend on Christmas morning.

Christmas Day is family time—time to revel in the interplay and interweaving of the three generations.

But there are yet the traditional Twelve Days of Christmas, divided in two by New Year's Day. The stories will continue, and the family will celebrate by visiting, playing games, sharing good times, traveling, etc. As

the end of the year approaches, it will be time to gather together and debrief about the year that is ending. What went best? Which things are remembered most fondly? Which ought to be best forgotten and never repeated? Of all the books or stories read, music listened to, plays or films observed, jaunts or trips taken, which ones are treasured most? Out of all this mix resolutions for the coming year will flow naturally. Midnight, December 31, will bring with it 365 days and nights of new opportunities to be of service in the lives of others.

Six more days of Christmas remain, each one more precious than the last because of their proximity to Epiphany, or Day of the Wise Men. In Catholic countries children often enjoy this eve and day most of all because on it the Wise Men leave gifts in their shoes.

On January 6 it will be time to take down the tree, restore the decorations to their storage boxes, tenderly place in their box the figures associated with the manger scene or crêche—and put Christmas away. But what wonderful memories will have been made before then! And it will be these memories that will elicit the longing question, "How many days till Christmas?"

Serenity. We have been describing at least 36 serene days and nights (52, if we incorporate the mid-November coming of St. Nicholas, as the Dutch do). Just imagine the impact upon our nation if each family were to shut out the world for one-seventh of each year! What an impact it would make on the minds, hearts, and souls of our children, not to mention the opportunity for harried adults to retreat to and regenerate in a quiet Eden of their own making. How much stronger they'd be, how much strengthened to face the challenges of the new year, come each January 7.

And then, if only we could bridge across the year to the next Christmas on piers of evensongs! (See "Evensong," the concluding story in this collection.)

The Eleventh Collection

We have set a daunting task for ourselves: each collection of Christmas stories ought to be the best yet. We think you'll agree that this one meets that expectation.

Of the authors our readers have grown to love over the years, none can compare to Margaret E. Sangster, Jr. "This Christmas Business" is the eighth of her stories to appear in the *Christmas in My Heart* series. (They appeared in books 2, 3, 5, 6, 8, 9, and 10).

But as we began our second decade, we wanted to stir in some new blood, so the other authors in book 11 are appearing for the first time. Without question, this year's headliner is Barbara Robinson's "The Best Christmas Pageant Ever," published first as a separate book by Harper & Row in 1972. It has since become one of the all-time Christmas best-sellers, selling in the millions. Readers will want to secure the complete book text.

We almost lost Gerald Toner's memorable "Lipstick Like Lindsay's." Since it anchors a book by the same title (which readers will want to get), it was mighty difficult for us to secure permission to include it. I predict this story will become one of the all-time great Christmas classics.

The oldest story? Unquestionably "Angela's Christmas," now more than a century old.

Robinson and Toner remind us that great Christmas stories are still being written. As do the inclusion of stories penned by Dennis Eberhart, Wilbur Hendricks, Ellen Austin, Lucy Parr, Arlene Anibal, Julie Rae Rickard, and Karen A. Williams.

Welcome to our second decade!

CODA

I look forward to hearing from you! Please do keep the stories, responses, and suggestions coming—and not just for Christmas stories. I am putting together collections centered around other genres as well. You may reach me by writing to:

Joe L. Wheeler, Ph.D.
c/o Review and Herald® Publishing Association
55 West Oak Ridge Drive
Hagerstown, MD 21740

May the Lord bless and guide the ministry of these stories in your home.

And the Two Were Made One

Dennis Eberhart

Never had he been angrier at the preacher than now. Why, the very idea of forcing upon his boys the two ugliest and scrawniest Christmas trees!

Only later did he hear the rest of the story.

It was one of those lazy, quiet, comfortable afternoons that come just before Christmas. Our home had been beautifully decorated, and all the necessary presents had been purchased, wrapped, and placed beneath the tree. My wife had decided to do some "extra" baking and was just putting a sheet of cookies in the oven.

I had been drafted to keep the grandchildren quiet and "out from under foot" until the first batch was cool enough to eat. As we settled ourselves on and around the sofa, a general clamoring went up for me to tell a story that has become a family tradition.

I was 21 years old and still in college. I had helped to pay part of my schooling each year by operating a Christmas tree lot on a vacant corner right near downtown. Business had been pretty good that year,

and I was in high holiday spirits when I saw the preacher and his two young boys walking up from their car. Each year I tried unsuccessfully to give them their tree. They not only insisted on paying but usually gave me more than I would have charged for their pick. And they would refuse to discuss it further with a smile and a backhanded wave of one hand.

You can imagine my surprise on this night when the preacher walked up to me and said, "John, we're here hoping to find two of the scrawniest, ugliest trees that you've ever seen!"

It was pretty plain that something was wrong, because the two young boys, who usually ran laughing and shouting from tree to tree, were now just staring at the ground without a word as they stood close by their father.

I shrugged at the preacher, saying, "OK, reverend, what's the joke?"

He said, "It's no joke, John. We're serious. This year we've decided to buy the two ugliest, scrawniest trees that you have."

"Well, all right then," I said as I walked to the back of the lot. "All the rejects are over here."

My heart sank within me as I led them to that forlorn pile of cast-offs. I sensed that for some reason, some reason that I didn't know, these boys were being punished for something that they'd done. This should have been a joyous occasion for two young boys, and it made me angry that it was being turned into some sort of object lesson. I wanted to punch that preacher in the nose, and I seriously considered calling him down. But it just wasn't right to argue with a man in front of his own children.

I picked two of the ugliest trees and twirled them around half heartedly. I was hoping that the pastor would make his point and let the boys get on with their real business.

"Ahhh, yes!" he exclaimed. "These are perfect for what we want, aren't they boys?"

The boys answered glumly with "Sure, Dad" and "Anything you say."

"OK, John," shouted the preacher. "Let's load 'em up!"

As I walked to their car I kept looking back and forth from those trees to the depressed looks on those kids' faces, and my emotions boiled over. *No one should be allowed to treat children like this,* I said to myself. *Especially at Christmas!*

While the preacher and I loaded the trees into the trunk of the car, the two boys climbed silently into the back seat. When I heard the car door slam, I grabbed their father by the lapel of his coat and dragged him out of earshot.

"Just what do you mean, stickin' those boys of yours with lousy trees like that?" I demanded roughly. I rarely called the preacher by his first name, but at the moment I wasn't sure whether he deserved my respect. "Listen, Bill," I said hotly, "if you're trying to punish those boys of yours for something they've done, I don't mind telling you that I think you're going about it all wrong!"

The preacher looked at me intently with raised eyebrows for several seconds. But then, as he reached down and gently took my clenched fist from the lapel of his coat, a twinkle came into his eyes and the trace of a smile played across his lips. With a tone of infinite patience in his voice, his soft answer turned away my wrath. "John," he said, "you've known me all your life. Now in all those years I want you to name one time when I've done something unfair or unreasonable to my wife or children."

As I thought back, time after time came to mind when I had questioned the preacher's judgment, only to find out later that the wisdom of years lay behind it. Without exception the pastor's solutions to problems were always the fairest to all concerned. And now, as I searched my mind, I couldn't think of a time when he'd been unfair to anyone, let alone his own family. I had to admit as much to him. But I couldn't keep myself from demanding (somewhat irreverently) to know what, in heaven's name, had been the boys' awful crime.

The preacher gently placed his hand on my shoulder. "John," he said, "do you know a girl named Margaret Johnson?"

I quickly made a mental search of all the faces that I'd ever seen and came to a stop at that of a girl I knew from school. She had long brown hair and would have been considered pretty if it weren't for the quiet, tired look in her eyes. She'd had few friends and kept pretty much to herself. Most everyone thought that she was kind of strange on account of the odd clothes she wore. She was always out of style. But I responded to the preacher's question with a simple "Yeah, she was in my class at school."

"Well," he continued, "I don't know if you're aware of it, but Maggie Johnson is old Sam Johnson's daughter, or at least one of them. There's eight kids in that family. Maybe you never knew old Sam—he was

killed in an accident down at the mill nine or 10 years ago. Ever since then, Mrs. Johnson has had to try to hold that family together by herself.

"And from my own experiences with them, I can tell you that it has not been an easy task. Every time the church has a rummage sale, there she is picking through all those old clothes that nobody else will have, trying to outfit those kids of hers. We've always tried to let her take whatever she wants, but she always insists on paying, same as anyone else!"

My mind raced back to Margaret Johnson's raggedy clothing in high school and how we all thought she was sort of weird. My anger had already been turned to humility, and now I was becoming disgusted with myself. I couldn't help wondering what Maggie must have thought about us. I tried unsuccessfully to swallow a lump in my throat.

"Where do your boys come into all this?" I asked weakly.

"I'm just getting to that," the preacher said. "Ever since graduating from high school Maggie has been working down at the mill, trying to help her mother with the bills and raising the rest of the kids. I don't have to tell you how hard mill work is, and I doubt if she spends a dime of her pay on anything extra for herself.

"I'm telling you, John, that's a girl to be proud of! And yet—well, the other day I was paying a pastoral call on Ralph and Hilde Evans over on South Main Street. As I stood on their front porch saying goodbye, I saw my boys and a couple of their friends walking behind Maggie. I suppose she was on her way home from work. Anyway, these kids were following her. And

appropriate party.

"Yes," the woman said with a heavy North Jersey accent. "I am familiar with that product. Did you say you are a lawyer?" I noted caution in her voice.

"Yes, I am. But please, this isn't business. I just want a tube for my little girl. I'll pay for you to Federal Express it—"

"Oh," she laughed, "four years ago we sold millions of those lipsticks. You know how fads go, though. Two years ago the market dwindled to nothing. We dropped the stuff. Listen, you don't want last year's news. This year it's glitter stickers. You can get 'em everywhere!"

Her words hit like the proverbial ton of bricks. "But Jennie doesn't want what every kid wants this year. You don't have maybe a few sticks left, you know, for old times' sake?"

"Take my word," she replied, "they're out. O-u-t, out!"

"Right, well, thanks for the information." I hung up. The big "NO" had come from the "Big Apple," and I realized that I was in considerable trouble.

That night my wife and I regrouped. She was the first to deal with the problem head on. "I'd say you are up the well-known creek," she said.

"I'd say you are right," I said.

"Well," she began after a pause, "maybe we should just let Jennie know in a note that Santa Claus tried as hard as possible, but that we can't always get everything we want."

"That's fine for Jennie," I chuckled weakly, though I knew it wouldn't be fine for Jennie, "but what about me?"

She looked at me solemnly, realizing for the first time how deeply this test of my traditional principle-agent relationship with Saint Nicholas had cut to my core. The conversation drifted, and I began to compose in my mind the note explaining why there would be no crayon lipstick like Lindsay Schell's.

Officially, the search ended that night. I am, after all, an adult of sorts. To anyone who asked at the office, I adhered to the party line: you can't have what isn't available.

Secretly, I continued to pursue every possible avenue as the days moved all too quickly toward Christmas. I called my sister in Cincinnati and my mother-in-law in Birmingham. After a few pleasantries I got to the point, mercilessly shaming myself and offering eternal gratitude if they could find the lipstick in Ohio or Alabama. They tried, but my operatives met with no success.

On my way to see a client in Frankfort I purposely took the long way through Shelbyville, hoping to myself that one of the old, small-town drugstores, ignorant of the outdated nature of the stuff, might have some of the crayon makeup left on a dusty shelf.

"We had some, dear," said the jolly little lady with the purple rinse in her hair, "but we sold out."

"I know," I said with resignation. "I didn't really think you'd have any."

She showed me another very nice lipstick, but I knew it would never do. I was 20 minutes late for my meeting, and I said I had been delayed by "business." As Marley said to Scrooge, "mankind was my business."

My efforts became calmer, more fatalistic. On December 23, when I went into the old Woolworth's that still remained in downtown Lexington, I was almost as

33

amused as they when I revealed that I knew some of their stock had been shipped over from Louisville.

"How did you know?"

"Oh, I get around," I said, feeling a little like a Fuller brush man. "Now, about the crayon lipstick . . ."

Like the kind man in Louisville had done, the lady walked me to the aisle where it had been and was no more. I thanked her, and walked back into the rain. For it was still raining.

I finished my business and headed north, out of town. I mentally reviewed my efforts and realized that I had covered more square miles in my search for the perfect present than during any other Christmas. I also realized that I had failed. The drizzle, which continued in a light but steady stream, fit my mood perfectly.

It was not the nature of the gift that prompted my frustration, nor my failure to attain its purchase that fed my melancholia. In years past and I was sure in years to come, I had reminded and would remind myself and my family—Jennie and, later, my son John—that the greatest gift Saint Nicholas would have us give or receive in Christ's name would be our love. Certainly baseball gloves, dollhouses, fur coats, gold jewelry, or even automobiles are merely second-class attempts at showing that love. The wise men knew that even as they came forth with their frankincense, gold, and myrrh.

It was more a sense of a failed entrustment that overcame me. Saint Nicholas had made me the trustee for his simple little gift to Jennie, and I felt as though I had somehow breached my fiduciary duty to both of them. I knew in my head that my wife's recommendation of a note that the lipstick's absence would be a helpful passage to matu-

rity, but in my heart there was no solace for failure.

These were my thoughts as I shifted into fifth gear and began to pass the Northland Shopping Center on my way out of Lexington. Out of the corner of my left eye I noticed the sign of another Begley's Drug Store, just like the one I had investigated in Shelbyville. I felt it was as good a time as any to buy the substitute lipstick, so I switched on my left-hand signal and pulled into the lot.

Wet, as usual (had I ever been dry?), I dripped into the store and began the now well-practiced craning of my neck to determine on which aisle I might find their stock of Bo-Po, Tinkerbell, and so on.

A heavyset woman in her late 40s came over to ask if I could be helped. By now a certain similarity of features had begun to emerge in the ladies who worked at the Begley's, Walgreen's, Taylor's, and other drugstores I had visited. Modified cat's eye glasses dangling from a gold elastic band, heavily rouged cheeks moving rhythmically with the cadence of her chewing gum, her hair coiffed in frozen perfection—this was the lady who stood before me asking, "May I help you?"

"I was looking for play makeup," I said. "Specifically, lipstick."

"We have some in toys," she began, pointing off to a spot at the back of the center aisle. I began ambling back to toys.

"We also used to have some on the hang-up displays over on the specialty racks."

I slowly turned, careful to contain my curiosity. "Did it, uh, have a little girl on the front and look like a crayon?" I asked, my mouth turning to Play-Doh.

"Sure did, honey. Let's see; follow me."

Nearly stumbling twice, I followed her to the far side of the store, beginning to babble incoherently about how I had been looking for this certain type of lipstick but couldn't find it, and if they had any, well, I would be very happy, but I would understand if they didn't, and so on. I'm sure I was saved from being heard, since she had gotten several steps ahead of me and was already thumbing through the pegboard displays when I caught up with her.

"Here we go," she said.

I stared in dumbfounded amazement as she went on.

"I'm sorry; I don't see the lipstick. I guess we sold out . . . But here's the nail polish . . . in cherry . . . strawberry . . . and here's cologne . . ."

I had never gotten this close before. Like a squirrelly bearded bookworm who has found a first edition of *Oliver Twist* on the dollar book shelf, I savored the mere sight of this now antiquated line of children's makeup. There was no lipstick, but perhaps this might be my substitute.

"I'm sorry the lipsticks are gone," she continued, "but we have all of these"—she didn't even change her tone of voice—"well, look what somebody has stuck back here on the wrong hook."

At that moment the blessing of Saint Nicholas descended upon Begley's Drug Store in the Northland Shopping Center and caused to appear before my very eyes the only unpurchased, fresh, and unopened package of crayon lipstick like Lindsay Schell's in the Commonwealth of Kentucky. My MasterCard would have been hers for the asking, but it was reduced for clearance to $1.37, and she held it out toward me. "Is this OK?" she asked nonchalantly.

I restrained the urge to embrace her on the spot and kiss away the rouge on her cheeks. "You do not know," I said slowly, trying to keep the lump down in my throat, "how you have helped to make my little girl's Christmas—and my own. I'll take it."

She smiled passively, not revealing if she knew just what I meant, or was perhaps slightly embarrassed at the Event she had stumbled upon.

I gathered up a modest collection of the remaining makeup and followed her in stunned joy to the checkout counter. I went on to ask her if there were any more lipsticks in the stockroom or at another store, and while she was kind enough to check for me, I needn't tell you that I had uncovered the last stick known to mankind.

The rain continued on my way back to Louisville, and neither cleared nor miraculously turned to snow by the time I got back home. I am but a crass human, agent for a greater principal for whom we joyfully toil at this time of year. Yet even I realized on the trip home alone, as I was reminded on Christmas morning when Jennie found her lipstick and held it gleefully upward for all to see, and again whenever I have thought about it since, that a Christmas trust had been fulfilled on aisle 1 of Begley's Drug Store that rainy December day. It had little to do with play lipstick—and everything to do with love.

_____

Gerald R. Toner, attorney and author, writes from Louisville, Kentucky. His short stories have appeared in magazines such as *The Saturday Evening Post, Ladies' Home Journal,* and *Redbook.* Among his published books are *Whittlesworth Comes to Christmas, Holly Day's Café and Other Christmas Stories,* and *Lipstick Like Lindsay's and Other Christmas Stories.*

At Lowest Ebb

Author Unknown

It was a bleak Christmas that year for the young pioneer minister and his wife. The money was gone, and even the well had given out. God, it appeared, had completely forgotten them.

But someone had forgotten to tell this to little Ruth.

I remember a day one winter that stands out like a boulder in my life. The weather was unusually cold, our salary had not been regularly paid, and it did not meet our needs when it was.

My husband was away much of the time, traveling from one district to another. Our boys were well, but my little Ruth was ailing, and at best none of us were decently clothed. I patched and repatched, with spirits sinking to the lowest ebb. The water gave out in the well and the wind blew through cracks in the floor.

The people in this frontier parish were kind, and generous too; but the settlement was new, and each family was struggling for itself. Little by little, at the time I needed it most, my faith began to waver.

Early in life I was taught to take God at His word, and I thought my lesson was well learned. I had lived upon the promises in dark times until I knew, as David did, "who was my fortress and deliverer." Now a daily prayer for forgiveness was all that I could offer.

My husband's overcoat was hardly thick enough for October, and he was often obliged to ride miles to attend some meeting or funeral. Many times our breakfast was Indian cake and a cup of tea without sugar.

Christmas was coming; the children always expected their presents. I remember the ice was thick and smooth, and the boys were each craving a pair of skates. Ruth, in some unaccountable way, had taken a fancy that the dolls I had made were no longer suitable. She wanted a nice large one and insisted on praying for it.

I knew it was impossible but, oh! How I wanted to give each child a present. It seemed as if God had deserted us, but I did not tell my husband this. He worked so earnestly and heartily I supposed him to be as hopeful as ever. I kept the sitting room cheerful with an open fire, and I tried to serve our scanty meals as invitingly as I could.

The morning before Christmas James was called to see a sick man. I put up a piece of bread for his lunch (it was the best I could do), wrapped my plaid shawl around his neck, and then tried to whisper a promise as I often had, but the words died away upon my lips. I let him go without it.

That was a dark, hopeless day. I coaxed the children to bed early, for I could not bear their talk. When Ruth went, I listened to her prayer. She asked for the last time most explicitly for her doll and for skates for her brothers. Her bright face looked so lovely when she whispered to me "You know, I think they'll be here early tomorrow morning, Mama" that I thought I'd be willing to move heaven and earth to save her from disappointment. I sat down alone and gave way to the most bitter tears.

Before long James returned, chilled and exhausted. As he drew off his boots the thin stockings slipped off with them, and his feet were red with cold.

"I wouldn't treat a dog that way, let alone a faithful servant," I said. Then, as I glanced up and saw the hard lines in his face and the look of despair, it flashed across me: James had let go, too.

I brought him a cup of tea, feeling sick and dizzy at the very thought. He took my hand, and we sat for an hour without a word. I wanted to die and meet God and tell Him His promise wasn't true. My soul was so full of rebellious despair.

There came a sound of bells, a quick stop, and a loud knock at the door. James sprang up to open it. There stood Deacon White. "A box came by express just before dark. I brought it around as soon as I could get away. Reckoned it might be for Christmas. 'At any rate,' I said to myself, 'they shall have it tonight.' There is a turkey my wife asked me to fetch along, and these other things I believe belong to you."

There was a basket of potatoes and a bag of flour. Talking all the time, he carried in the box, and then with a hearty goodnight he rode away.

Still without speaking, James found a chisel and opened the box. He drew out first a thick red blanket, and we saw that beneath was full of clothing. It seemed at that moment as if Christ fastened upon me a look of reproach. James sat down and covered his face with his hands. "I can't touch them!" he exclaimed. "I haven't been true, just when God was trying me to see if I could hold out. Do you think I could not see how you were suffering? And I had no word of comfort to offer. I know now how to preach the awfulness of turning away from God."

"James," I said, clinging to him, "don't take it to heart like this. I am to blame; I ought to have helped you. We will ask Him together to forgive us."

"Wait a moment, dear, I cannot talk now," he said. Then he went into another room.

I knelt down, and my heart broke. In an instant all the darkness, all the stubbornness, rolled away. Jesus came again and stood before me, but with the loving word "Daughter!"

Sweet promises of tenderness and joy flooded my soul. I was so lost in praise and gratitude that I forgot everything else. I don't know how long it was before James came back, but I knew he too had found peace.

"Now, my dear wife," he said, "let us thank God together." And he then poured out words of praise—Bible words, for nothing else could express our thanksgiving.

It was 11:00, the fire was low, and there was the great box, and nothing touched but the warm blanket we needed. We piled on some fresh logs, lighted two candles, and began to examine our treasures.

We drew out an overcoat—I made James try it on— just the right size. And I danced around him, for all my lightheartedness had returned. Then there was a cloak, and he insisted in seeing me in it. My spirits always infected him, and we both laughed like foolish children.

There was a warm suit of clothes and three pairs of woolen hose. There was a dress for me and yards of flannel, a pair of Arctic overshoes for each of us. In mine was a slip of paper. I have it now and mean to hand it down to my children. On it was written Jacob's blessing to Asher: "Thy shoes shall be iron and brass, and as thy days so shall thy strength be." In the gloves (evidently for James) the same dear hand had written: "I, the Lord thy God, will hold thy right hand, saying unto thee: Fear not, I will help thee."

It was a wonderful box and had been packed with thoughtful care. There was a suit of clothes for each of the boys and a little red gown for Ruth. There were mittens, scarves, and hoods. Down in the center was a box. We opened it—and there was a great wax doll. I burst into tears again. James wept with me for joy. It was too much. And then we both exclaimed again, for close behind it came two pairs of skates. There were books for us to read (some of them I had yearned for), stories for the children to read, aprons and underclothing, knots of ribbon, a gay little tidy, a lovely photograph, needles, buttons, and thread, a muff, and an envelope containing a $10 gold piece.

At last we cried over everything we took up. It was past midnight, and we were faint and exhausted with happiness. I made a cup of tea, cut a fresh loaf of bread, and James boiled some eggs. We drew up the table before the fire, and how we enjoyed our supper! And then we sat, talking over our life, and how sure a help God had always proved.

You should have seen the children the next morning! The boys raised a shout at the sight of their skates. Ruth caught up her doll and hugged it tightly without a word. Then she went into her room and knelt by her bed.

When she came back she whispered to me, "I knew it would be here, Mama, but I wanted to thank God just the same, you know."

My husband then said, "Look here, wife, see the difference?"

We went to the window, and there were the boys out of the house already, skating on the ice with all their might.

My husband and I both tried to return thanks to the church in the East that had sent us the box and have tried to return thanks unto God every day since. Hard times have come again and again, but we have trusted in Him, dreading nothing so much as to doubt His protecting care. Again and again, we have proved that "they that seek the Lord shall not want of any good thing."

Christmas Love

Ellen Austin

Why couldn't her husband understand that she didn't want to share him with anyone else? After all, it was their first Christmas together!

Against her wishes, he finally persuaded her to go to Aunt Betty's house. But she wouldn't know a soul there.

Glen, my husband, surprised me by saying, "Ellie, let's go to Wilsonville. I want you to spend Christmas in Aunt Betty's house."

"You're joking," I said in dismay. "I've decorated the apartment for our first Christmas together. Besides, your hometown is a thousand miles away and tomorrow is Christmas Eve. Your Aunt Betty's certainly not expecting us . . ." I stopped because I was out of breath, not because I'd run out of reasons why we shouldn't go.

"We can start now, drive all night, and be there tomorrow afternoon," Glen replied. "Ellie, I want Aunt Betty to meet you. She'll love you as much as I do." He said it with such sincerity, and his little boy grin had the same appeal that had attracted me to Glen when we'd first met. I found myself saying, "All right. We'll go to Wilsonville for Christmas."

But even as I locked the apartment door behind us I didn't feel right about it. We'd been married only six months, and this Christmas was special. I loved Glen too much to share him with anyone. Didn't he feel the same way about me?

The lights of the city twinkled like the bulbs on a Christmas tree as we started for Wilsonville, and I thought of the little tree we'd left behind. I'd shopped during a week of lunch hours before I found the *right* tree. I'd rushed home after work to assemble it, and by the time Glen came through the door I had it decorated. It added sparkle to the corner of our tiny living room.

"You're going to like Christmas at Aunt Betty's," Glen said, breaking into my thoughts. "I hope you'll get to meet all seven of my cousins. They're scattered now, but they all try to come home for Christmas. And you can learn a lot about love from Aunt Betty."

The car radio played a modern version of "Jingle Bells" and Glen hummed along. I felt a wave of irritation. I didn't need Aunt Betty to teach me how to love Glen. Because I had Glen I felt that I didn't need anyone else, least of all Aunt Betty and a houseful of cousins.

"I don't know why I agreed to go to Wilsonville," I said. "I really wanted to spend Christmas in the city, all alone with you, in front of our little Christmas tree."

"But honey, we've been alone in front of that tree. Now I want my family to meet you, and I want you to know them. You might say that this trip is my Christmas present to you."

Glen didn't understand. He was mine now; our marriage vows said so. How could he belong to me and his family?

The possible answer to that question frightened me.

39

Fear gnawed at me all the way to Wilsonville, and by the time we stood in front of Aunt Betty's door I felt miserable.

Then I was engulfed in Aunt Betty's firm hug and she was exclaiming over me and congratulating Glen. "Well, it's about time Glen finally shared you with his family," she said, as if she'd known we were coming.

I'll admit I was surprised by the welcome they extended to me. The house was full with seven cousins and their families, yet there was plenty of room for us.

I found myself the center of attention as cousin Norma showed me the family coat-of-arms and told me great-grandpa Sommers had come from England. Cliff and Patty told stories about Glen when he was a little boy. JoAnn loaned me her sweater when we went after wood for the fireplace, and Mason explained the family ritual of decorating the tree after supper on Christmas Eve.

I became a part of the family ritual that night. The freshly cut tree stood in the middle of Aunt Betty's living room. Each member of the family attached hand-made decorations to its fragile branches—decorations made over the years by Aunt Betty's children and carefully stored in a closet.

With Glen by my side, I stood with the others as we joined hands and formed a circle around the tree to sing old, familiar carols. Then they sang to me a carol I didn't know. "Love came down at Christmas . . . love be yours and love be mine . . ." (the words were by Christina Rossetti, 1830-1894). Their faces were softened by the lights of the tree as they smiled at me.

"Welcome to the family, Ellie," Aunt Betty said. My heart seemed to be so filled with love for all of them that I felt I really loved Glen more than I had before.

"I repeat the same words every Christmas, because they're still true," Aunt Betty was saying. "Christmas helps us to remember that love grows when it is shared. The more love we share, the more we have to give. May the love of Christmas fill our hearts and remain with us all through the year."

"Merry Christmas, Ellie," Glen said softly, smiling down at me. Suddenly I knew why Glen had wanted me to spend Christmas at Aunt Betty's home.

"It's a wonderful present," I said to Glen, and I squeezed his hand as we stood beside the tree. "Thank you for helping me to understand Christmas Love."

Ellen Austin wrote for popular magazines during the second half of the twentieth century.

40

The Christmas Doll

Author Unknown

Christmas was almost upon her, and Marty yearned with all her nine years of tomboy-hood for the silver skates in Grover's store. She had no interest at all in silly girl stuff and could more than hold her own in sled races with any boy in town.

But then came a visitor with the hateful name of Rodney.

And then came something else in Grover's front window.

I t was three days to Christmas and the ice skates and the hockey stick for Miss Martha Jones lay on the top shelf of the front closet, pushed well back and cunningly concealed by her father's raincoat.

Marty moved the coat just enough to assure herself that what lay underneath was what she had ordered—or rather, requested. She was not a bossy child, although at 9 her pigtails, round face, and solid body gave her a bold look of confidence that intimidated nervous adults.

Satisfied that it was safe to boast about what she was getting, Marty climbed down and went into the kitchen where she had left her ski jacket and an apple, then shouted into space that she was going sliding.

From upstairs her mother, whose mouth was full of pins, shouted back with muffled good temper that this plan was acceptable, and would Marty please get home in time for dinner.

"What's dessert?" Marty yelled, weighing her answer.

"Apple pie."

Marty paused in the act of putting on her jacket and contemplated her apple. There would be one apple fewer in the pie, but that was life. "I'll be back in puh-lenty of time," she shouted reassuringly. "Where are my mittens?"

"In your pocket."

This turned out to be true, and one of them, in fact, was stuck to a half sucked sourball. Marty worried the sourball loose and stuck it in her mouth. "Well, g'bye," she said briskly, and shot out the door.

She paused to get her sled, and then, singing "Hark the Herr-uld Angels Sing" at the top of her lungs, she bounced happily toward Hudson Hill. It was perfect sliding weather, just cold enough, and she could see her breath puffing importantly before her into the bright clear air that smelled of snow and Christmas.

The hills, when she arrived, were swarming with that deceptively aimless activity peculiar to anthills, subway crowds, and children at play. Marty lifted her sled and clutched it firmly to her middle. Then she gave a loud cry, somewhat reminiscent of one of the

Valkyries on a good day, and shot off recklessly downhill.

The cold air blew in her face and rushed down her throat since her mouth was open to shout "Hallelujah! Hallelujah!", which seemed very appropriate to the holiday season and made very good shouting. For a moment she owned the hill, the town, and the whole world, all in one burst of dizzy white speed. No one could fly so fast or so far as Marty Jones, except maybe God's angels.

"Hallelujah!" shouted Marty, addressing the angels with hearty reverence. "Hallelu—" She broke off in midglory, her mouth ajar. The unthinkable had happened. A sled and rider had rocketed past her at breakneck speed. Marty gave a violent heave and pressed herself flatter, urging her sled to take wings and meet the challenge, but it was too late. She arrived at the base of the hill a good two yards behind her competitor and came to a stop by dragging both feet. The owner of the rival sled rose from his glistening red and yellow chariot and stood looking down at her, his hands in his pockets.

He was a new boy she had never seen before, about her own age, chunky, with a button nose and cowlick of brown hair plastered to his forehead by snow. He said a hostile "Ya-ah."

"Yah yourself," Marty said. "Bet you can't steer as good as I can."

"I c'n steer rings around you with both hands tied behind my back," he informed her, and to show his superiority further, he spit grandly through a gap in his front teeth.

She eyed him jealously. "You lose a tooth?"

"Got knocked out in a fight."

This was an advantage beyond all argument. Marty herself had never qualified for a fist fight since boys were always checked by some primeval sense of etiquette, probably batted into them by their mothers, and girls refused to fight at all. Marty returned to the attack. "What's your name?"

"Rodney," he said, and added "Anderson" after a pause.

"Rodney's a fatheaded name," Marty said pleasantly. "Mine's Marty Jones."

"Fathead yourself," Rodney said.

The amenities dealt with, they fell into a brief silence. At this moment a third sled suddenly appeared, and its rider fell off into the snow with a resigned cry. It was Tommy Egan, and he always fell off, some inscrutable providence having shaped him like a butterball without any adhesive surfaces. Like the White Knight, he had acquired a fine ability for talking upside down, whether in a winter snowdrift or a summer blackberry thicket. What he was announcing this time was that Rodney was his cousin.

"Ho," Marty said gratefully, as this explained Rodney. He was visiting. Briskly she whacked the snow off Tommy's rear with her mitten and told him that she and Rodney had already met.

"I beat her coming down the hill," said Rodney.

"You did *not*," said Marty, spirited, if inaccurate.

Rodney eyed her distantly. "I'm going to get a new sled for Christmas," he said.

"My parents," said Marty loftily, "are giving me ice

skates and a hockey stick."

"Like fun they are," said Rodney. "Girls can't play hockey."

"Marty can," Tommy said loyally.

Rodney grunted. It was one of those superior masculine grunts that are calculated to drive an independent female mad. It worked fine on Marty. "I'll show you exactly the kind of skates they're buying me," she said importantly. "They're in the window at Grover's store, and they've got rawhide laces and everything. And there's a hockey stick goes with 'em."

"Huh," said Rodney. "My parents would give me anything in that old store window that I wanted, I guess."

"So would mine," Marty said quickly.

"They would not."

"They would so."

Tommy, who had a pacific nature, said, "You can show him the skates on the way home, Marty. We can go round by Grover's."

"All right, I will," Marty said, and she gave herself and her sled a flounce that faced them uphill. "Betcha don't dare go down the other side of the hill."

Tommy looked at her anxiously. "Through the trees?"

"Sure, through the trees." She poked a finger at Rodney. "You don't dare."

"I dare anything once."

"Yah, coward custard," said Marty. "I dare anything twice." She started uphill with her sled. Rodney glared and girded himself for battle.

By the end of an hour they had arrived at a stale-

mate. On the home ground Marty had a wider way with tree trunks and overhanging branches, but Rodney had a system all his own of streaking straight for peril and then hauling his sled back on its tail like a plunging mustang. Tommy was aghast. Each downhill flight convinced hm that it would be their last, and he had carried them off to the hospital and broken the sad news to their parents so many times that at last even his fertile imagination tired, and he sat quietly on his sled like a small, stout, and sympathetic snowman.

It was Rodney who, with calm superiority, said he guessed Marty must be tired by now, being a girl. Marty's chin jutted out dangerously. Tommy reminded them they were going to stop by Grover's. Marty grunted, jerked her sled around, and led the way, while in her mind's eye she skated victoriously to some distant goal line, wielding her Christmas hockey stick as Rodney labored to catch up, his ankles sagging.

Grover's store shone out at them through the early December twilight. Even from a distance they could see the Christmas tree in the plate glass window, brave with lights and dripping tinsel, the mysterious red-ribboned package clustered at its base, and all about it that wonderful, star-dust, plum-pudding, carol-chanting look that is both wild and holy, and not possible for any other month or any other tree.

Marty savored the richness. The skates would be lying near the tree, their runners reflecting in its glittering ornaments. She tasted the flavor of saying casually, "That's the kind I'm getting." Then, as she looked she gave a yelp of dismay. The skates were gone, and in their place, crowning frustration, there was a doll!

Marty's eyes, blind to dolls, skimmed over this one and lighted on a catcher's mitt, newly introduced and indicating that Grover's was not lost to all sense of decency. If there had been less snow around she might have coveted the mitt, but her mind was on skates, and baseball could wait for spring. She muttered at the window and turned to scowl at the doll.

It was different from other dolls, being neither a blonde nor vacuous-looking. It had brown hair and a serene look, and it was wearing an old-fashioned dress with lace collar and cuffs. Black-strapped slippers showed just below the hem.

After a minute Tommy poked Marty with his elbow. "There's your skates," he said. "Under the tree."

"She's stuck on the doll," said Rodney.

Marty turned around and gave him a look of fury. "I am not! I was looking at the catcher's mitt." She pointed firmly to the skates. "Those are mine," she said.

Rodney admitted grudgingly that they weren't bad.

Marty didn't hear him. She was staring into the window again, and after a moment she pulled one of her braids around and began to chew fiercely on the end of it. Something inside her was stretching out its arms to the doll, and she felt a dreadful melting-down sensation. She said gruffly, "What'd they want to put a silly old doll in the window for?" and knew that she had hurt the doll's feelings.

Dolls didn't have feelings. She must be crazy.

Marty gave a sudden blood-curdling whoop, whirled her sled around, and announced to the world that the last one back to her house was a black-eared baboon. Tommy said, "C'mon, Marty," with no more hope of making a successful protest than a corporal reasoning with a general. Rodney had already leaped into action, but Marty caught up with him at the first lamp post and cut in front of him so neatly with her sled that he fell into a snowbank

The incident restored her morale and cleared her head of fancy emotions so that she forgot the doll. Greatly cheered, she went into the house, which was full of the good hot smell of cinnamon and apple.

Her father accepted her hug placidly and pulled a pigtail. Her mother, whom she encountered in the kitchen, observed that she was trailing melted snow all over the house and shooed her upstairs. With a comfortable sense of being extremely welcome, Marty shook off her snow pants in the middle of her room, started to pull off her sweater, and paused on the fourth button.

The doll was back, tugging at her thoughts.

Still unbuttoning absentmindedly, she went over and sat on the bed. Her room was messy but austere, and there was no place whatever in it for a brown-haired doll in a lace-trimmed dress.

Well, it could go on top of the bed—it wasn't absolutely necessary to have a life preserver marked S.S. *Algonquin* on her pillow. The life preserver could go under the bed, and the doll could—

"Oh, yah!" Marty said furiously to the empty room. "Yah, yah, yah!" What would everybody think if it got out that Marty Jones was hankering for a doll? That little pipsqueak of a Janie Darrow had told her once to act more ladylike, and Marty had kicked her hard right in the rear of her fancy pink dress. Suppose Janie Darrow saw her with a doll?

She didn't want a doll. She didn't want a doll! She wanted her skates and hockey stick.

Comforted by her vehemence, Marty dropped down on the bed and lay with her nose in the pillow. Tonight they would decorate the tree, and on Christmas Eve her skates would go under the wide branches. With a card with her name on it. No Santa Claus nonsense. Marty had distrusted his whiskers from the age of 2.

In her mind's eye she began to unwrap the skates. She unwound the red ribbon, pushed aside the crackling tissue paper, looked at the white shiny cardboard of the lid, waiting to be lifted. She lifted it

Inside was the doll.

Marty sat up with a terrible snort and smacked her feet down on the floor. Fugitive from dreams, she ran to her closet, snatched a pair of grubby overalls off a hook, and put them on. They were the toughest looking things she owned, and she felt a vast need for toughness. She didn't want the doll. She never had wanted a doll, and she never would want a doll. That settled that! She clattered downstairs to dinner.

Mr. Jones gazed at his daughter with a kind of awe. "What did you do all day, squirt?"

"Coasted," Marty said. "Tommy Egan's cousin is visiting him. He really stinks."

"Marty!" The upward inflection in her mother's voice was a reproach on the choice of words.

"Smells," Marty amended primly. "His name is Rodney, and he thinks he can beat me sliding."

"Ah." Mr. Jones nodded comprehension.

"We came back past Grover's," Marty said compulsively. "They've put a doll in the window."

"Dolls," Mr. Jones said broadmindedly, "are not essentially vicious."

Marty thought of the brown hair to be stroked, the lace collar and cuffs, and the tiny strapped shoes. "Dolls stin—"

"Marty!"

"I don't like dolls."

"Very sad," said her father. "We bought you one for Christmas."

For just a second Marty's heart gave a magnificent leap, then she realized her father was teasing. She solaced herself with two helpings of pie. It wouldn't have been the doll anyway.

"Marty, you'll bust."

"Are we going to trim the tree tonight?"

"As soon as the dishes are done."

The moment they'd finished them, Marty dragged her parents into the living room. "First, the star," Marty said. "The star on top." She held it up with reverence. It was silver, sprinkled with bright specks. It was a Wise Men's star, fit to be stationary in a sky of great importance on a night of great light, and Marty always felt a little holy when it finally got into place on top of the tall green tree.

The red balls came next, then the blue, the silver, and last, the gold, trembling and bowing at the tips of the branches. Then the special ornaments: a woolen Santa Claus that Marty didn't like, but that had been on Marty's mother's tree when she was a baby, and therefore, had seniority rights; an angel with gold wings, a halo, and an expression of impressive vacuity;

a peacock-like bird of great dignity and poor balance; and, finally, Marty's favorite, a rainbow ball caged in glittering silver and powdered with gold.

By the time the tinsel hung in glittering loops from star to carpet, the whole room was lighted up with Christmas. "Every year we do it better," Marty said solemnly.

She sat down on the floor, hugging her knees and contemplating the star-crowned achievement. On Christmas Eve her parents would put their present for her under the tree, and she would be allowed to poke it. Even though she knew what was inside, there would be that pleasantly tingling feeling of anticipation. You could get that feeling just looking at the space under the tree where the package would be.

She looked at the space hopefully, and nothing happened. This was one of the best moments of Christmas, and nothing happened at all. Marty rested her chin unhappily on her knees. It wasn't just because she knew beforehand what her present would be; she almost always knew that. And she wanted the skates; she wanted them terribly. Only this morning she had been in a passion of joy at the thought of them.

The doll rose uninvited in her mind, lovable beyond any reasonable dream. Marty closed her eyes and said "Nebuchadnezzar" under her breath, trying to exorcise the doll with strong words, but it was no use. She opened her eyes. All her life she had been all of a piece, and now there was a stranger inside her, a stranger who wanted a doll. "Darling," Marty said softly, making the doll welcome, ashamed to be saying it and helpless not to.

Someone tapped at the window. She whirled around and saw the tip of a round nose pressed hard against the pane. Armed in the righteousness of invaded privacy, Marty stalked to the front door and yanked it open.

"Hello," Tommy said sociably. "We're going to the store for ice cream. Can you come along?"

"Nope," said Marty, "it's too late. I wouldn't be allowed."

Rodney waded up off the snowbanked lawn. "She's not old enough to go out by herself," he explained loftily to Tommy.

"I'm as old as you are!"

"You're a girl."

"Is that so?" said Marty, raging. "I can beat you running, I can beat you sliding, I can beat you at anything."

Rodney said, "I'm going skiing tomorrow. I'm going down Hudson Hill on skis."

Without stopping to think about it, Marty said, "So'm I."

Rodney briskly told her not to be silly. "You can't ski."

"I can so!"

"You cannot. Tommy says you don't know how."

"Tommy doesn't know everything," Marty said darkly, implying that she had led a life of great danger in the Alps.

"It just happens," Rodney said casually, "that I'm going to ski down the other side of the hill."

"Don't pay any attention to him, Marty," Tommy said earnestly. "He's kidding."

"Who's kidding?" said Rodney. "I'm not scared of any old hill."

"I'm not either," Marty said quickly. "Anything you can ski down, I can, too."

"Huh. You haven't even got skis."

This was true, but her father had a pair. They were in the basement, near the collection corner where she kept various things such as the large bone that her father generously agreed might have belonged to a dinosaur.

"I'll take my father's skis," Marty said grandly.

In technical possession of the field, she swaggered back into the house and started upstairs, looking over her shoulder for just a moment at the tree with its trembling shower of tinseled light and the bright glitter of the Christmas balls reflecting the room in endless enchanting miniature.

She took the stairs two at a time and sang while she put on her pajamas. A general feeling of good will, based on the routing of Rodney, enveloped her. Her father's skis would undoubtedly be too large, but that hardly mattered.

Her father's skis!

About to leap into bed, Marty stopped and sat down on the edge of it. After a moment she drew her feet in, pulled the covers over her and, hunching up, stared at the opposite wall.

She must have been crazy to tell Rodney she would take her father's skis. Suppose she busted them? It was perfectly possible, since she'd never been on skis before. It wouldn't help much to tell her father that Rodney had dared her.

What on earth had got into her? There must be

something wrong with her. She curled up tight and buried her head in the pillow. The whole thing was the doll's fault. She'd only bragged to Rodney to prove to herself that she wasn't the kind of dope who wanted a doll. She hated the old thing. Nothing had gone right since she had seen it in the store window. If she had it here now she would smash its head.

The image of the doll rose in her mind and looked at her pleadingly. Marty hardened her heart. She would have none of it; she would show it she didn't care. Tomorrow, first thing, she would go look into Grover's window, and the doll wouldn't interest her a particle. Not one tiny little measly bit. Deliberately, coldly, she pushed it out of her mind—the lace-trimmed dress, the white hands and the little feet, the brown hair.

After a moment not thinking about the doll became quite easy, and she felt a sort of sleepy triumph. She would make the doll let go of her, and rid of it, she would be herself again, all of a piece. Her mind drowsed, slid deliciously into a picture of herself on skis flashing in and out of trees, while Rodney stood by in amazement and chagrin. The whole problem began to fade to misty at the edges, then dissolved. Marty gave a little growl of hope and comfort, rearranged herself, and slept.

There were muffins for breakfast the next morning, and the Christmas tree looked beautiful. Marty announced that she was going down to the village. "I hafta," she said firmly.

"Well, if you hafta, you hafta," her mother said. "Don't stuff yourself so, Marty; the muffins won't get away."

Marty had just pushed a buttery one-half into her mouth and at the same time reached for reinforcements. She grinned amiably, indifferent to etiquette, and when she left the house she had two emergency muffins in her pockets.

The good crisp air pleased her. She felt strong and superior, last night's optimism and this morning's muffins making a firm foundation inside her. She was Marty Jones, with no invisible fidgets.

Grover's came in sight. She put her hands nonchalantly into her pockets, hit a muffin on each side, and pulled one out. Chewing like a calm cow, she walked up to the window. Her eyes swept it with cool detachment and came to rest immediately on the doll, its skirts spread, its hands folded in its lap. Marty's heart turned over. She clutched her muffin in helpless love. She pressed her nose against the glass of the window, and through the frosty "O" of her breath could have howled from pure frustration and longing.

A voice said, "Hullo, Marty," and she spun around, choking down adoration and muffin. It was Tommy—and Rodney, of course. They were following her around. In silence she began chewing savagely on her second muffin.

"What are you doing?" said Tommy.

Marty said distantly, "I had an errand. At the grocery store." She hated them both. They were always making her tell fibs.

"What were you looking at?"

"Nothing," said Marty.

Tommy, who liked speculation, waved a hand at the window. "If you could have anything you wanted in the window, what would you take?"

It was generally a good game, but this time it wasn't. The doll looked at Marty in a waiting sort of way. "The catcher's mitt," Marty said stoically. It was like hitting a kitten across its nose, and it was no good telling herself that the doll didn't have any feelings. She glared at Rodney.

He spit through the gap in his front teeth in a businesslike way. "When you going to take your father's skis?"

"Right now," said Marty, hating him. She turned on her feet.

"See you at the hill," said Rodney.

Instead of going in shouting by the back door, Marty let herself quietly in through the basement. Totally unpracticed in secrecy, she was clumsy about it, but she had no choice because if her mother saw her taking the skis, there would be considerable trouble. Marty did not approve of having trouble with parents. They were right, in general, and in this case they would be right in particular. It would be hopeless to try to explain.

The skis were heavy and her feet dragged, taking her to the hill. Maybe Rodney had changed his mind.

He hadn't. He was already there, waiting for her, with Tommy a faithful shadow. The three of them made a silent procession to the other side of the hill.

With Tommy's help, Marty laid her skis out funerally. "They're too big for you," Tommy said.

Marty nodded. The fact seemed like a reproach, a reminder that the skis were not for her. She turned them carefully toward the brow of the hill before she put them on. Rodney kept eyeing her impatiently, but it was all right for him. His skis fit.

Safely mounted, she took her first real look at the hill. She knew every twist and turn of it, and the trees were no more than a bright challenge. From skis, though, it looked altogether different. The sudden coldness in her hands was not winter's. She caught her breath and took a quick look at Rodney.

"Scared?" he asked.

"In a pig's eye," Marty said, using a frowned-upon expression to stiffen her knees.

"Well, go ahead, then."

"Go ahead yourself."

"You don't know how to ski," Rodney pointed out. "I don't want you running into me from behind."

Tommy said, "I don't see why either of you have to go down." But his was a lost cause.

Marty swallowed hard. She shuffled her feet forward and found her knees trembling so bad that they would hardly support her. It was because she was afraid she might damage her father's skis. She knew, hopelessly, that it wasn't that way at all. She was just plain scared, the way any sissy would be. The way Janie Darrow would be, or any silly girl who played with dolls. It was bad enough to have shown off by taking a stupid dare in the first place, but to be frightened now was unforgivable. She was face to face with the true Marty Jones at last, and it was not to be endured. At least no one was ever going to know that she was scared!

With a fierce cry Marty thrust herself forward over the brow of the hill. She heard Rodney's shout—or it might have been Tommy's—and she saw the tree coming at her, distant and black and narrow for an astonishingly long time, and then suddenly so close that the deep-ridged bark was like a map with rivers on it. If she had been on her sled she would have known just how to twist and scrape lightly past. But the skis refused to turn, no matter how her feet wrenched at them. The tree refused to move. The map with its rivers became bigger than the sky.

Marty yelled and tried madly to kick off her father's skis so they wouldn't break. The rivers rose up spectacularly. A big, bright, black star exploded with a crash and split itself into a million comets.

The world spun itself quiet.

* * *

Dr. Grosby said cheerfully, "Abrasions, concussion, and lacerations." Even from a great dreamy distance Marty recognized his voice and then her mother's asking anxiously, "Is she all right, Dr. Grosby?"

"Mrs. Jones," Dr. Grosby said, "children are indestructible. Where did you come from, baby dear? Out of the rock pile into there?" He started to make packing-up noises. Marty flickered her eyelids cautiously. "Stop peering at me, Marty," he said sternly. "Your mother's worried about you. Sit up and show her you're all right."

She sat up, and she was all right except for her head, which swam. He put a nice, large, cool hand on it and smiled unexpectedly. "All right, Tarzan, lie back again. I'll drop by tomorrow, Mrs. Jones. Keep her in bed. If necessary, tie her down."

Mrs. Jones smiled. The doctor left. After a moment Marty said, "Mum," in a small voice. "What happened to the skis?"

"One of them broke."

Marty carefully smoothed the top of her sheet over the blanket. "It wasn't a very good idea to take them, was it?"

"I've heard better ideas." However, her mother gave the blanket a pat, and the blanket included Marty. "Go to sleep now. I'll pull the shades."

Marty slid down against the pillow, closed her eyes, and slept instantly. She awoke in a twilight room, sat up in bed and yelled, "Mother!"

Her mother put her head around the door. "You've got visitors, Marty. Rodney and Tommy. Do you want to see them?"

"Sure, send 'em in," Marty said regally, and she assumed a consciously heroic pose.

When the door opened again it was Tommy who sidled around it, his round face expressing concern. After him came Rodney. Rodney's expression was glum, and he was carrying a box.

Marty eyed it with curiosity. Rodney said, "My aunt says I shouldn't have dared you to go down that hill. She says to tell you I'm sorry."

"It's all right," said Marty, languid and queenlike.

"I brought you a present," Rodney said, still glum, and shoved the box toward her. Grover's Department Store was written on its lid.

The catcher's mitt, Marty thought. It was Rodney who maintained that girls couldn't play baseball. Triumph tasted sweet in her mouth. She broke the string and lifted the box cover.

The doll stared up at her. It was dearer, more lovely

even than she had remembered it. It lay in its nest of tissue paper, smiling gently, and with its arms reaching out in the serene confidence of being welcome. Marty's hands reached out too, and then stopped. She couldn't let them go to the doll. Not in front of Rodney. She pushed the box away from her, not rudely, but just enough to show how little she cared. The doll still smiled.

And all of a sudden something inside Marty stretched and grew tall. She knew now that she loved the doll and that the doll loved her. Who cared what Rodney thought? She took the doll firmly out of its box and, holding it close to her, looked at Rodney over its head. Her mouth was a tight line and her chin stuck out. Silently she dared him to jeer at her.

Rodney said, "My aunt picked it out for you. I told her you'd rather have the catcher's mitt but she said no." His face was no more scornful than the doll's. "Would you rather have the catcher's mitt, Marty?"

Marty shook her head. "I like the doll," she said. "I like the doll a whole lot."

He looked puzzled but relieved, and she decided there was no use trying to explain. She loved the doll, and when she got her skates on Christmas morning under the star-tipped tree, she would love them, too. Loving the doll was simply a new part of herself that she hadn't met before. Marty felt a warm interest in the discovery. It was like opening a package. Sometimes you knew what was inside, and sometimes you were surprised. It was all rather unexpected, like Christmas itself, but like Christmas, it was also very rich and secure.

She held the doll tight in her arms and bent her head to impress a kiss on the round, sweet cheek. The kiss, however, was interrupted by a novel sensation. Marty raised her head. "Hey, you know what?" she said happily. "I think I must've knocked a front tooth loose. I'll be able to spit."

She knew her friends would be very happy for her—with a loose tooth and a new doll on the same day.

You Are Never Too Old

Myrtle Edna Rouse

Uncle Matt stormed out of the house. No one—not even gentle Aunt Sally—was going to stop him from telling that bantam rooster of a lawyer a thing or two! Not even if Christmas was at the door.

Aunt Sally could only pray that God would put His hook in her husband's nose and turn him around.

Little did she know . . .

Can't teach an old dog new tricks, you say? Oh yes, you can! You can teach him a great many things. Just let the lesson be sharp and decisive enough and he will learn. I am reminded of that every time I think of Uncle Matt's squabble with Lawyer Banton.

I remember that evening as if it were yesterday and can see the cheerful kitchen—living room, it usually was on winter evenings. Farm folks went to bed so early that it seldom seemed worthwhile to light the fire in the front room heater. Anyway, the kitchen was the best room in the house—glowing and vital with all the vigorous living that went on under its high-beamed ceiling. The floor was spread with newspapers where the boys were busy greasing their heavy boots, getting them in readiness for the first winter weather. Aunt Sally sat in her "walking chair," with her knitting needles clicking busily. We called her old rocker the "walking chair" because it did just that when she rocked in it.

Aunt Sally was one of the gentlest women alive. She never scolded or nagged. Her speech was sometimes seasoned with salt, to be sure, but it always showed forth that grace that the true Christian is admonished to possess. When she was worried about something we usually learned about it by the vigor with which she would start her chair to rocking. And then the old rocker would walk. Sometimes, as she wrestled with the inner woman, she would travel clear across the kitchen and find herself face to face with the wall in the corner behind the back door. Then she would rise soberly, pull the chair back to its accustomed place, and sit down to start the proceeding over again, never seeming to realize at all what had happened.

When Uncle Matt was present he would catch hold of the back of the chair when it started on its journey. "Whoa there, Sally. You're goin' to rock yourself clear off the farm someday. Don't want to lose you, girl!"

Auntie would smile sheepishly and answer, "I was just thinking."

"Powerful thoughts," her husband would tease. "I'm glad you keep 'em to yourself!"

But this night Aunt Sally seemed at perfect peace. Her face was serene and happy, and her fingers flew over the warm red wool in her lap. Under the radiant circle of the lamp I was wrestling with my first problems in long division, and Uncle Matt, as usual, had thrown himself down on the rather disreputable old sofa and covered himself with the gay afghan that Aunt Sally had knitted especially for him. His wife was just opening her lips to say, "Now, Matt, why don't you just go to bed? You'll be asleep there in a minute."

But Uncle Matt was getting up. He pulled on his high boots, took his warm jacket from the hook, and reached for his gloves where they were drying on the top of the warming oven. He was going out—and the hands of the old clock already pointed to half past eight! Here was something new indeed. Everyone in the room was startled into instant alertness.

"Just thought I'd take a little walk before I turn in."

But his wife was not fooled for a moment. An anxious look crept into her eyes. "Matt, please don't go and stir up trouble with that lawyer."

The look that Uncle shot at her from under his shaggy black brows was far from placid. Why did Sally have to be so discerning? It was almost as if she read a man's mind.

"I told you I wasn't goin' to pay that bill, and I'm not! The case never went to court. And him sendin' me a bill for his services! Why, he didn't have to do nothin'! And he acted quite put out because me and Jim got together and settled things between us. Why, Jim and me's been friends—boy and man—for nigh on to 40 years. I guess we can fix things up between ourselves if we want to. Oh, I know," he continued as Aunt Sally showed signs of attempting to break in, "he's a smart man. Thought of things about this case that I never dreamed of myself. We'd have licked Jim hands

down if the case had come up—but it's better this way. What are you so wrought up about? You never wanted me to have the law on Jim in the first place."

"Of course, I didn't. It was all a lot of foolishness, and I knew you'd be good and sick of it before long. But Matt, you ought to pay this young man his money. He did earn it. You know he made several trips out here, and he had to do some paperwork and write a lot of letters. It isn't his fault that you didn't go through with the case. Think, Matt, how disappointing 'twould be to a young fellow. You know, having a good case, one where he knew he could make a showing for himself, and then having it all taken out of his hands. Right when he's trying to make a start in this town, too! He's not asking very much, Matt, please—"

They were an incongruous pair as they stood there. Aunt Sally was small and plump as a partridge, and Uncle Matt big and broad, with muscles of iron. But no matter how he might rave or how angry he might appear, Aunt Sally was never afraid of him. She stood her ground now until her husband's eyes fell before hers. Then he slammed out of the house with a parting challenge: "I'm going to tell that lawyer that I don't owe him one cent. And if he gives me any argument I'll—" His mumbled threat was lost outside when he slammed the door.

Uncle Matt was addicted to profanity, and Aunt Sally had often held her hands over her ears through some of his expletives, hustling us youngsters out of the room in short order. But we had listened from the hall with our ears pressed close to the crack of the door. Aunt Sally was different from the neighbor women about swearing. Profanity among the men folks was quite taken for granted, and although no cultured woman used it and youngsters had their mouths washed out with strong soap if they said bad words, the fact that the men cursed freely both at home and abroad caused them no concern.

But as I said, Aunt Sally was different. Of all the things she bore from her really kindhearted husband, this caused her the most pain. She often remonstrated with him in her gentle way, and even took him to task more severely when his expletives were especially offensive. Uncle Matt never was angry during these scoldings. He would laugh rather shamefacedly and promise to do better in the future. But when he lost his temper again he forgot all about his good intentions.

When the banging of the door had ceased to echo through the house, Auntie called us back into the kitchen for prayers. She had prayers with us every evening, and Uncle Matt made no objections. He would lie on the couch and listen with good humor to the Bible story, but he always seemed to fall asleep before we had prayer.

That night I clung to Aunt Sally, sobbing. "Is Uncle Matt really going to do something dreadful to Lawyer Banton?"

"There, there, child. Don't cry. Of course not. We are going to pray about it right now."

We did pray. I still can see that grieved yet determined look on my dear little auntie's face as she prayed, what seemed to me, a strange and rather terrible prayer. "O Lord, rebuke Matt for his blasphemy against Thee. Put Thy hook in his nose this night and turn him around."

A hook in his nose! Wasn't that going too far? I loved Uncle Matt, and my tears were about to break out afresh. But there was something about Aunt Sally's face that seemed to preclude questioning just then, and I went silently to bed—but not to sleep.

I thought about young Robert Banton and his wife, Mary. They were my ideals. Of course, I knew neither of them except by sight and through hearsay in the village, but I loved them both a great deal. When does romance awaken in a girl's heart? Perhaps it is born there. Robert Banton was my knight in shining armor and Mary was the beautiful princess in the tower. Her wild rose loveliness and her handsome husband were not too hard to fit into their roles, either. He was more than stalwart and good looking, as befits any knight. He was the one whose strength was as the strength of 10 because his heart was pure.

You will laugh when you hear how I got that idea, but it will serve to show you what big thoughts little girls sometimes think, and how much they are able to grasp from grownups' talk. Things perhaps of which the grownups are scarcely aware.

I had heard Uncle Matt say to Aunt Sally, "Don't see how that young lawyer that's courtin' Mary Hathaway is goin' to get any place. Every time you see them they've got her ma along. I was telling some of the boys today that I can't make up my mind whether he's courtin' the girl or her ma."

It was said jokingly, but the little pitcher with the big ears picked it up and it registered. There was something about this that pleased the grown folks. This was the way nice people did things. Somehow it was different from the way they thought and spoke of Hattie Simms, who was always going out with different young men and getting home late from parties. Oh, this was the way my own shining knight would be when he came riding by.

Mary had always been almost a legend in the village. She was wonderfully sweet to look upon. And there was more, a sort of inner beauty and graciousness, that set her apart from everyone else. Carefully trained and cherished by a widowed mother, she exemplified the highest ideal of taste and refinement of which our village could boast. And with it all, she was so friendly and natural that even the girls, whose mothers were always admonishing them to be like Mary Hathaway, could hold no resentment.

Her young suitor was not a local product. Our boys either settled down on the farm, following their fathers in some occupation in the village, or went into the lumber camps in the woods. If a boy did leave the beaten path and seek a place in one of the professions, he did not come back to the little country town. Thus, the villagers were pleased when this personable-looking young man came among them, all prepared to practice law.

And now he and Mary were married. They had a small but shining house on the right side of the tracks, and Robert had an office over the bank. They had no horse and buggy, and Robert's overcoat was too thin for the rigors of winter in that section of the country. But however hard getting started in a profession was in those days, they kept their troubles to themselves, and everyone considered them quite the darlings of fortune.

If you owed money to the grocer, you paid it. A man could not hold up his head in the community unless he paid for what he ate, and everyone knew that the grocer had to have money. How else could he keep his shelves stocked with provisions? But the lawyer, and even the doctor, were different. They could always be expected to wait.

Of course, I did not think of all these things that night. I did not even know them. I just lay there and trembled for my gentle knight and waited for Uncle Matt. Robert Banton might be as brave as any knight that ever rode in days of old, but I knew that he was no match for Uncle Matt. Why, there was no one in all the country who could match his strength! What was he even now doing to bring distress to the little white house under the evergreens? And I was worried about him, too. What if the Lord should take Aunt Sally seriously? Uncle Matt might be ever so big and strong, but if God took things into His hands I knew Uncle Matt would not have a chance. I did wish that Aunt Sally had not prayed just like that!

And then I heard the kitchen door open and Uncle Matt come in. I tumbled over to the stovepipe hole as quietly as I could. That was a leftover from the time when Aunt Sally had the kitchen enlarged, and to me, at least, it was a great convenience. Uncle Matt was standing just inside the door—and he had had a hook in his nose all right. That was easy to tell. He mumbled that Sally should have been in bed long ago, and before the astounded woman could do more than gather up her knitting, he crossed the floor in great strides and blew out the lamp. Then they were feeling their way past my door in the dark. I heard him say, "Hit my nose against

the porch pillar somehow."

And Aunt Sally said in a strange little voice, "That so, Matt? That's too bad."

She came in after a while to see if I was covered up warm, and I put my arms around her and said in a frightened whisper, "He did it all right! Oh, Aunt Sally, God put a hook in his nose!"

She didn't hear me at first. Then she buried her face in the covers and her shoulders shook. Of course, I thought she was crying—she couldn't have been laughing, could she? After a few minutes she straightened up and wiped her eyes. "What are you talking about, child? Who did what?"

"Your prayer, Aunt Sally. Don't you remember? You said, 'Put a hook in his nose.' Oh, poor Uncle Matt—what will happen to him now?"

Aunt Sally's face was very thoughtful. "I did say that, didn't I? And yes, God did—but you have no cause to worry, child. God loves your Uncle Matthew. And if He put a hook in his nose you can make up your mind that that is just the very best thing that could happen to him. You go to sleep, lamb. This is going to do your uncle a pile of good."

Things were very quiet around the

house for the next few days. Uncle Matt was as sheepish as Rover was the time we caught him sucking eggs. Of course, I knew what had happened to him, but the boys were skeptical. "But something sure is peculiar. He hasn't even said a swear word, around the house at least, for almost a week! Do you suppose he's had his mouth washed out with soap?"

And that night around the supper table we had another surprise. Several of the neighbor men had been working in our wood lot, and Aunt Sally had asked them in for supper. Replete after one of her good meals, they were lounging comfortably back from the table, engaging in the sort of "man talk" that the youngsters found so thrilling. And as was customary, many a swearword was mixed casually into their conversation.

Uncle Matt was as nervous as a trapped coyote. He kept wandering around the room from stove to cupboard to door until Aunt Sally looked up from her dish washing in astonishment. Finally he burst out, "Do you men have to swear every second word? My wife doesn't like swearin' and—I mean—she doesn't have to listen to it. Not in her own kitchen."

Well, it broke up the party, to say the least. After a few uneasy words of farewell, the men departed in stunned silence. But their amazement could not have been half so deep as our own. Later in the evening Uncle Matt looked up from his paper and smiled wistfully at his wife. "Guess I surprised you tonight, Sal. Wonder if the whole community is goin' to be mad at me. I like all the boys, but why do they have to—"

(We had begun to notice the strangest blanks in Uncle Matt's language).

Aunt Sally looked at him with sparkling eyes. "Don't you worry, Matt. They'll get over it. I was proud of you tonight!" Her middle-aged cheeks were flushed like a girl's. "It makes a woman feel like a queen to have her man take up for her."

"I guess it does—I never realized—I mean—I'm not goin' to swear anymore, either in the house or outside. Cursin' is a silly business." He reached over and patted her hand, and for a little while there was silence, broken only by the tick of the clock. Then he went on with a chuckle. "Never told you about what happened when I went to see Lawyer Banton the other night, did I?"

"No, you didn't." Aunt Sally was all eagerness, and you can imagine that we children pricked up our ears too.

"Well, Sally, he threw me out of the house."

"Ooh, he never did!" Her voice sounded amazed but not too displeased at the idea and, strangely enough, Uncle Matt sounded pleased himself.

"Remember what a purty snowstorm we was havin' that night? Well, when I stamped the snow off my boots on the front porch of that dollhouse, I looked in at the homiest little picture a man could ever hope to see. There was a gay little Christmas tree in the window, and her and him was at the piano singing carols. She had a long dress on, and her hair on the top of her head, and"—Uncle Matt was very much in earnest—"'cept for you, Sally, she was the purtiest girl I ever laid eyes on.

"I hated to barge in on 'em and was just turnin' away when they swung the door open and urged me inside. Well, I floundered around some, but I finally stated my business, just like I said I would. The lawyer took exception to it, same as you had done, and put up about the same arguments. They made me mad. Of course, I knew I was wrong, Sally, but you know how obstinate I am. I began to let go good and strong. At the first swearword Lawyer Banton said, 'Mr. Moore, my wife is present.'

"I thought that was a mite peculiar. After all, I had met the Mrs. when I first came in. But I turned again, as polite as I could under the circumstances, and said, 'Good evening.' Then I went right back to tellin' him where I stood, in no uncertain terms. Couldn't he understand that I had already lost money on the deal by halfway givin' in to Jim? I couldn't afford to hand out money to him besides. I don't remember just what I said, but of course there were swearwords mixed up in it. It had quite an effect on the young fellow. He got to his feet—mad clear through I could see, but as quiet and polite as before.

"'I don't want your money, Mr. Moore, but this is my home. No man can come here and, in my wife's presence, use the language that you have been using.' He swung the door wide. 'Now get out!'"

Uncle Matt paused, and we waited with bated breath. "Honest, I never even thought of disputin' him, Sally. I was sort of bewildered. It was the first time any man had ever ordered me out of his house, and I leaped awkwardly to my feet, knockin' over a little table and dear-knows-what knickknack in the process. It made quite a commotion. And the girl's mother, who lives with them and who is pretty frail-lookin' these days, came hurrying in from the other room, crying, 'Be careful, Robert! He's going to—' But it was the slip of a girl who really took the wind out of my sails. Bless her little

heart. I can hear her yet!

"'Don't hurt him, Bob! Oh, please don't hurt him!'

"She meant it, too. It was like a shot in the arm to the young whippersnapper. You know what you said about feeling like a queen, Sally? Well, I guess Lawyer Banton felt like a king right then. And I—I felt like a yellow dog! Even if I'd wanted to I couldn't have started anything after that. Perhaps her husband thought I wasn't goin' to go, for he caught me by the shoulder and propelled me through the door—with no gentle hand. And as luck would have it, I skidded on the icy step and banged face-first into the post of the veranda. You see, I didn't tell you any lie about the way I got my bloody nose.

"Mrs. Hathaway had the door locked quicker than you'd believe possible, and I heard her say, 'No, Robert, I won't give you the key. That man might—'

"And the little woman said, 'Oh, Bob, dear, let him go! Don't say anything more to him. After all, he is a much older man. But—oh darling, you were wonderful!'

"He answered, 'Let me go! I just want to see what happened to him. I didn't mean—' I got to my feet and got out of there—fast. I started for home, and then as soon as the cut on my nose stopped bleeding, I turned around and went back. When I came past the corner of the house I could hear their voices from the opened bedroom window.

"'I'm glad you told that dreadful man that we didn't want his money.'

"'That's all very fine,' was the response. 'But it just so happens that we *do* want it very much. It was what I was counting on to see us through Christmas. Without it there just isn't enough—even for much of a dinner.

Oh, darling, why must I have to stint you so when I want to give you everything?'

"Her voice was very low and sweet, like the crooning of a young mother over her baby. 'Bob, don't ever feel like that. I'm so happy just to have you, for the two of us to be together. What's a Christmas dinner? Why, I'll make some of that bread pudding you said was so good, and we'll have baked potatoes. Things will get better soon. You're going to be a very famous lawyer someday, Bob. I just know it!'

"About that time I knocked on the door, and Mr. Banton came to answer it in robe and slippers. I didn't feel much like talking, so I just said 'Good evening, Mr. Banton' like I hadn't even been there before that night. 'I've come to pay you the $25* I owe you and to tell you that Sally and me is expectin' the three of you for dinner on Christmas Day. I'll be here for you with the sleigh along about noon. Tell that little wife of yours that that "dreadful man" begs her to please come, and that he's goin' to make her eat them words.'"

"Oh, those poor children!" Aunt Sally came back to reality with a start. "My land! And Christmas is the day after tomorrow! Do you suppose they'll come, Matt?"

"Of course, they'll come. Bob said they would. And he wrung my hand like he was really glad things was all fixed up. He's a real man, that lad, and I take off my hat to him. Guess I can't call him 'that young bantam' anymore, not after him throwin' me out of the house, so to speak. And the girl—you'll love her, Sally! She isn't much older than our Judy would have been if she had lived. And she had the kind of love and loyalty for her man that I would have wanted our girl to have—the kind you've always given me. I thought about that on the way home that night and how I was always botherin' you, swearin' around, and all. Believe me, if Lawyer Banton's wife is too good for that sort of thing, my wife is too! Well, that's the story, girl. What do you think of it?"

"It is the most wonderful thing I have ever heard in my whole life, Matt. And not even beautiful Mary Hathaway is as happy as I!"

Myrtle Edna Rouse wrote for family and inspirational magazines early in the twentieth century.

---

*About $1,000 in 2002 currency.

Two Red Apples

Author Unknown

Christmas was going to be bleak indeed at the Widow Stevens' home—not even apples or oranges could she afford. All she had was love.

But Jimmy was permitted to look into Mrs. Black's beautifully decorated window. And it was here that the trouble began.

Widow Stevens lived on the outskirts of the city with her two children, Judy and Jimmy. She had been confined to her bed for weeks because of ill health. On the day before Christmas she called the children to her bedside.

"Sit down on the bed," she said, patting a spot close to her. I want to talk to you. I've been pretty sick, as you know, and haven't had the chance to get out and earn money."

Judy's brow wrinkled in concern. "Are you going to die, Mommy?"

"Oh, no, Judy, I'm not going to die." Mother smiled and kissed her forehead. "In fact, it won't be long before I'm well enough to get up and work again. But right now, well, I'm afraid there won't be any Christmas presents."

"That's OK, Mother," Jimmy said. "Merry Christmas anyhow."

"You're such good children," Mother said proudly. "I do wish we could have had some apples at least, and maybe some oranges. But there is one thing I can give you that doesn't cost any money—and that's my love. All my love to both you children."

So you see, although Judy and Jimmy didn't have many of the nice things we take for granted, they did have perhaps the most precious gift of all—their mother's love. And both children felt very special because of it. Still, Jimmy, being the man of the family, wished he could do something to make this Christmas memorable. If he could just manage to get two apples—one for Judy and one for Mother—he would feel satisfied. But how could he ever do it?

Later that afternoon Jimmy was watching the snowflakes drift down silently outside the living room window. By and by he noticed the Christmas tree in Mrs. Black's window across the way. She already had the lights on, even though it would be several hours until dark.

"Mother," he called out, "may I go across the road and see Mrs. Black's tree? It looks so pretty."

"All right," Mother agreed. "That would be something fun for you to do while Judy is napping, but don't bother Mrs. Black. Stay out on the road. In fact, you can walk down the road and take a look at all the decorations, if you want."

"Oh, boy!" squealed Jimmy, and before it seemed possible for a boy to put on coat, mittens, hat, and boots, Mother heard the front door bang behind him.

Jimmy looked at the tree from the road for a while, but it seemed he just could not resist going a bit closer. The enormous house itself was enough to make one stare spellbound, but it was the sparkling beauty of that tree that almost made him catch his breath. It was *so* gorgeous! Without realizing it, he crept up on the porch, and then to the window. With his nose pressed to the pane, he suddenly realized that the Blacks were having a party. Several children were playing games in the front room. And then he noticed something on the floor beneath the tree.

"Apples!" he said almost aloud. "And look at all those presents! Boy, would Judy love those things."

Suddenly the front door opened, and the butler, looking very cross, called, "Boy, get away from that window. Go on! Get away unless you want trouble."

As the door slammed shut, Jimmy did move back a few feet. But seeing the happy children around the tree inside, he soon forgot and found himself back at the window again. He crouched down, hoping that no one inside would notice him. But evidently someone did, because after a while Jimmy felt a firm hand take hold of his collar and lift him up, and he found himself staring into the face of a policeman!

"So you're the trespasser!" exclaimed the officer. "What are you doing here?"

Jimmy gulped hard. "N-nothing, sir."

The policeman lowered Jimmy to the porch floor. "You'd better come with me," he announced.

"Yes, sir." Jimmy's mouth felt dry, and his knees were shaking.

All the way to the station in the patrol car Jimmy's mind was in a whirl. What would Mother say? How long would they keep him at the station? Oh, how he wished he had remembered Mother's warning about not going too close to the house. Suddenly he blurted it all out. "I just wanted to see Mrs. Black's tree because we don't have a tree this year. My mother is sick, and we don't have any money. I was just wishing I had two of those red apples under the tree for Mother and Judy. She's my little sister."

The policeman glanced at his passenger. "And what do *you* want for Christmas?"

"Just those two apples, then I'd be happy," he said.

The policeman looked away quickly and swallowed hard. He didn't say anything until they reached the police station. "Now then, Jimmy, I'd like for you to come into the station for a while so we can get this thing straightened out."

Something about his manner told Jimmy he had nothing to fear. Once inside the station the policeman asked the boy to wait in a room for a few minutes. Then, walking into the dispatch room, he picked up the microphone.

"Sam," he said to the controller, "throw all the switches open, will you? I have a message here for all cars."

"All set," Sam answered.

"Attention all cars and police personnel. This is Officer Clancy of station number four. A few minutes ago I received a call to investigate a prowler. When I got there, I found a young boy, about 8 or 10 years old, looking in through the window at a party going on inside. He was admiring the Christmas tree and decorations. He wasn't hurting a thing—all he was doing was admiring and wishing, as most of us do at Christmas time. And do you know what he was wishing for? A bicycle? Lincoln logs? No. He was wishing for two apples. Just two apples—one for his sick mother, and one for his little sister. Nothing for himself, not even an apple. Now, I have this boy here at the station house. I'll keep him here another 45 minutes. So if there are any of you who have an extra apple hanging around that you want this lad's mother or sister to have, please bring it over here. I repeat, bring it to station house number four. That's all."

When Officer Clancy put the microphone down he looked over at Sam, who was wiping his eyes. "I'm going in to keep Jimmy company while we wait," Clancy said. "If an apple or two comes in from any of the boys, keep them, OK? We'll give them to the lad all at once." Sam smiled an enormous warm smile. "Sure, Clancy," he said.

About 45 minutes later, Officer Clancy emerged from the room where he had been visiting with Jimmy. He looked around quickly, and his face fell—there wasn't an apple in sight. Just then he saw Sam. "Hey," he called, "don't tell me nothing came in!"

Sam's face was a picture of pleasure. "Come here, Clancy. I want to show you something."

Clancy was still concerned. "It'd better be good."

"Open that door," Sam directed.

Clancy was startled when he peered through the

door. "Has there been a raid, or something? Two paddy wagons. A fire truck. Officers from all the stations! What goes on here, anyway?"

"Open the paddy wagon door!" Sam was as eager as a child.

When Clancy opened the door, what he saw almost took his breath away. "Why . . . why, there's *four bushels* of apples in there. And groceries!"

"Yes," grinned Sam, "and the other wagon is full of toys!"

"You mean, all of this is the two red apples I asked for?"

"Yes," said Sam again. "And that isn't all. Look here."

"Money!" gasped Clancy.

"Seven hundred and ninety dollars, to be exact." Sam flipped the bills in his hand.

"But—but—." Clancy sputtered. "It wasn't more than 45 minutes ago that I put the call out—and now all this!"

"Ah, my dear Clancy," said Sam. "When you touch the heart of a city, even as big a city as ours, things begin to happen."

"But I only talked over the police radio," interrupted Clancy.

"Yes," nodded Sam. "But it seems a reporter for the *Chronicle* was listening in. And you know reporters. Before you could bat an eye, he was in touch with the radio and television stations, and the entire city heard your speech almost word for word. And the result? Well, you're looking at it. What do you think of it?"

Words simply would not come to Clancy. He was too overwhelmed.

Sam pointed to the fire truck. "That's to lead the parade to the boy's house, and the mayor himself is on his way to ride in it."

Well, you can imagine the rest. There was the most wonderful procession to Jimmy's house that the city had ever seen. Jimmy and the mayor waved to everyone along the way from atop the shiny fire truck. People lined the streets to smile and call out "Merry Christmas" to Jimmy, for nearly the whole city seemed to have heard about Officer Clancy and Jimmy and the two red apples.

Angela's Christmas

Julia Schayer

This Christian Herald story is one of the oldest stories in this collection: more than 100 years old. It is set in the dark and desperate London that Dickens immortalized, a world where girls and women had mighty few options, especially if they were poor. And even more especially if they were pretty.

Old Marg had once, ever so long ago, been young and pretty. Pretty like the lovely young woman welcoming in the derelicts, the down-and-outers, from the bitter cold.

Old Marg snarled.

Then it is 'yes,' Father dear?" said Angela, looking across the breakfast table with a smile. It was her mother's smile, and the girl had filled her mother's vacant chair for more than a year.

The eyes of the father and daughter met, and Angela knew, before a word was said, that she had conquered.

"I hate to see you at your age beginning to worry over these things," Ephraim Frazier said regretfully.

"Let the *old* women take care of the charities, dear. You keep on dancing in the sunshine a while longer, daughter."

Angela's smile grew graver but not less sweet. "I am 20, dear," she said. "Too old to dance *all* the time, and I cannot help *thinking*, you know. And—it's no use, Papa dear! I must do something! It *is* 'yes,' isn't it?"

"You are sure you won't mind being criticized and ridiculed?"

"Quite sure!" answered Angela.

"And sure you won't take your failures and disappointments to heart too deeply?"

"Quite sure I can bear them bravely," answered the girl. "If only one, *just one*, of those poor creatures may be helped and lifted up and brought out of darkness it will be worth trying for!"

"And what does Robert Johns say about it?"

A glow kindled in Angela's face. "Robert is in perfect sympathy with me," she said softly. She rose and went around to his side to speak with her face against the old banker's smoothly shaven cheek. "It is 'yes,' isn't it, Daddy dear?"

"Well, yes! Only you must go slow, dear. You are not over strong, you know."

And soon it came to pass that on a vacant lot hitherto given over to refuse heaps, haunted by stray cats, ragpickers, and vagrant children, in one of the vilest quarters of the metropolis, there sprang up with magic swiftness a commodious frame building, surrounded by smooth green sod, known in the lower circles as the Locust Street Home, and in upper circles laughingly denominated "Angela's Experiment."

Angela did not mind. It was mostly good-natured laughter, and many of the laughers ended by lending willing hands and hearts to the cause. It was wonderful how the news spread through the city's byways that here was a sanctuary into which cold, hunger, and fatigue dared not intrude; a place which the lowest might enter and be made welcome and go unquestioned, his personal rights as carefully respected as though he were one of the Four Hundred.

That was Angela's theory. No man, woman, or child should be *compelled* to anything. First, make their bodies comfortable, then surround them with ennobling influences and examples, entertain them, arouse them, stimulate them, hold out the helping hand, *and leave the rest to God.* "They shall not even be *compelled* to be clean!" she said, laughing. "If the beautiful clean bathrooms and clean clothing do not tempt them to cleanliness, then so be it! I will have no rules, only influences. You will see!"

And people did see, and wondered.

Sometimes on warm, pleasant evenings the spacious, cheerful hall, with its tables and chairs, would be almost empty. But on nights like that on which this story opens, a dark, cold December night, the seats were apt to be well filled, mostly with slatternly, hard-featured women and dull-faced children, who sat staring stolidly about, while the music and speaking went on, half stupefied by the warmth and tranquility so foreign to their lives.

Outside a dismal sleet was falling, but from the open door of the vestibule a great sheet of light fell upon the wet pavement, and above it glowed a transparency bearing the words: "A Merry Christmas to all! Come in!"

It was while the singing was going on, led by a high, sweet girl's voice, that a human figure came hobbling out from a side street and stopped short at the very edge of the lighted space. By her dress, it was a woman, an old, old woman, with a seamed, blotched face; an ugly, human wreck, all torn and battered and discolored by the storms of life. Such was old Marg— "Loony Marg," as she was called in the haunts that knew her best. Her history? She had forgotten it herself very likely, and there was no one to know or care—no one in the wide world to care if she should at any moment be trampled to death or slip from the dock into the black river. The garret that lodged her would find another tenant, the children of the gutters another target for their missiles. Not that she was worse than others. Only that she was old and ugly and sharp of tongue, and the world—even *her* world—has no use for such as she.

For some time this forlorn creature continued to hover on the edge of the lighted space. The sleet had become snow, and already a thin white film covered the pavement, promising "a white Christmas," and the cold increased from moment to moment.

The woman drew her filthy shawl closer. Her jaws chattered, yet she seemed unable to tear herself from the spot. Her eyes, alert as a rat's under their gray brows, were fixed now upon the open door, now upon the transparency, yet she made no motion toward the proffered shelter. Two men, hirsute and ragged, stopped near her and, after a moment's consultation, slunk across the square of light and disappeared into the building. As the door was opened there came a fuller burst of song and a rush of warm air, fragrant with the aroma of coffee and oysters.

The old woman's body quivered with desire. Food, warmth, rest—all that her miserable frame demanded—were there within easy reach, for the mere asking—nay, for the mere taking. Yet the devils of stubbornness and spite would not let go their hold upon her. Finally, as a bitter blast swept the snow stingingly against her face, she uttered a hoarse snarl and, glancing about to see that no jeering eye was upon her, the poor creature crept across the pavement, clambered up the stone steps, and, pushing open the door, slipped into the nearest vacant seat.

The chairs and benches were unusually well filled. Numbers of women and children were in the foreground. A few men were also present, sitting with their bodies hanging forward, their hats tightly clutched between their knees, their eyes fixed on the floor. The women and children, on the contrary, followed every movement of the young women on the platform with furtive eagerness.

The simplicity of attire that Angela and her friends had assumed did not deceive even the tiniest gutter child present. These were "ladies," and one and all accorded them the same tribute of genuine, if reluctant, admiration.

Old Marg, after the embarrassment of the first moment, took everything in with one hawk-like glance—the Christmas greens upon the clean, white walls, the curtained space in the rear that hid some pleasant mystery, the men and women on the platform.

At the organ sat a young girl, leaning upon the now silent keys, her face toward the young man who was speaking. Old Marg could not take her eyes from this face—white, serious, sweet, set in a halo of pale golden hair. The sight of it aroused strange feelings in the bosom of the old outcast. Fascinated, tortured, bewildered, she sat and gazed. It was long since she had thought of her youth. This girl reminded her of that forgotten time. Like a violet flung upon a refuse heap, the thought of her own innocent girlhood lay for an instant upon the foul mass of memories accumulated by 60 miserable years. *I was light-haired, too!* ran old Marg's thoughts. *Light-haired an' light-complected, like her!*

The perfume of that thought breathed across her soul and was gone. Still she gazed from under her shaggy brows and, without meaning to listen, found herself hearing what the speaker was saying. He was telling without rhetoric or cant the story of Christ, and with simplicity and tact presenting the lesson of His life.

"This joy of giving, of sacrificing for others," the young man was saying in his earnest, musical voice, "so far beyond the joy of receiving, is within the reach of every human being. Think of that! The poorest man or woman or child who breathes on earth tonight may know this joy, may give some pleasure, some help, some comfort, to some fellow-creature. Whether it be a human creature or a dumb beast matters not. It is all one in God's sight, being an act of love and kindness and sacrifice."

Old Marg looked down upon her squalid rags, her rough features writhed with a scornful smile. "That's a lie!" she muttered. "What could the likes of *me* do for anybody, I'd like to know!"

Still she listened; but at last, as the warmth stole through her sodden garments and into her chilled veins, and the peace of the place penetrated the turbulent recesses of her soul, the man's voice became like a voice heard in a dream, and the old outcast slept.

* * *

A confused sound greeted her awakening. Someone was playing the organ jubilantly. People were moving about—girls with trays loaded with steaming dishes. Children were talking and laughing excitedly. The curtain had been drawn, and a great Christmas tree almost blinded her with its splendor. She stared about in bewilderment. She looked at the tree, at the people, at her own foul rags. A fierce revulsion of feeling swept over her. Rage, shame, a desire to get out of sight, to be swallowed up in the darkness and misery which were her proper element, seized and mastered her. She staggered to her feet. A young girl approached her with a tray of tempting food. The sight and smell of it goaded the starved creature to madness. She could have fallen upon it like a wolf. Instead, she pushed the girl roughly aside and fumbled dizzily at the door-knob.

A hand was laid upon her arm. The girl with the sweet, white face was looking at her with a friendly smile. "Won't you stay and have something warm to eat before going into the cold?" the girl asked gently.

Old Marg shook the hand from her arm. "No!" she snarled. "I don't want nothin'! Let me go!"

With a patient smile Angela opened the door. "I am sorry you will not stay," she said softly. "It would give me great pleasure. There is a gift for you on the tree, too. It is Christmas Eve, you know!"

A hoarse, choking sound came from the woman's lips. She pushed by into the vestibule. Angela followed. "If you should feel differently tomorrow," she said, in her kind, gentle voice, "come here again, about 11:00. I shall be here." Without waiting for a reply, she reentered the hall. A young man, the same one who had been speaking, met her at the door.

"Angela!" he exclaimed. "You should not be out there in the cold!"

She smiled absently. "Did you see her, Robert?

"That terrible old woman? Yes, I saw her. A hopeless case, I fear."

Angela's eyes kept their absent look. "It was awful to see her go away like that, into the cold and snow, hungry and half-clad!" she said.

The young man leaned nearer. "Angela," he whispered. "You must not let these things sink into your heart as you do, or you cannot bear the work you have undertaken. As for that old creature, it is terrible to think of her, but she seemed to me beyond our reach."

"But not beyond God's reach *through us!*" said Angela.

* * *

Meanwhile, old Marg was facing the storm with rage and pain in her face and in her heart. The streets were deserted and lighted only by such beams as found their way through the dirty windows of shops and saloons. From these last came sounds of revelry and contention, and at one or another the poor creature paused, listening without fear to the familiar hubbub. Should she go in? Someone might give her a drink to ease for a time the terrible gnawing at her breast. Might? Yes; but more likely she would be thrust out with jeers and curses, and, for some reason, old Marg was in no mood to use the caustic wit and ready tongue that were her only weapons. So she staggered on until the swarming tenement was reached, stumbled up the five flights of unilluminated stairs, and almost fell headlong into the dismal garret that she called her home.

Feeling about in the darkness, she found a match and lit a bit of candle that stopped the neck of an empty bottle. It burned uncertainly, as if reluctant to disclose the scene upon which its light fell. A smoke-stained, sloping ceiling; a blackened floor; a shapeless mattress heaped with rags; a deal box;* a rusty stove resting upon two bricks, supporting in its turn an ancient frying pan, a chipped saucer, and a battered tin can from which, when the scavenger business was good, old Marg served afternoon tea. Such were her home and all her personal belongings.

There was no fire nor any means of producing one, but upon the box was spread a piece of paper containing a slice of bread and a soup bone, whereto clung some fragments of meat—the gift of a neighbor hardly less wretched than herself.

The old woman's eyes glittered at the sight and, seizing the food, she sank weakly upon the box and began gnawing at it. But her toothless jaws, stiff with cold, made no impression upon the tough meat and hard crust. Letting them drop to the floor, the poor creature fell to rocking to and fro, whimpering tearlessly, like a suffering dog. Strangely enough, within the withered bosom of this most wretched creature, there had welled up from some hidden source of womanly feeling a passionate self-pity, a no less passionate self-loathing. This was what a moment's contact with all that she had so long abjured—purity, order, gentleness—had brought to pass.

That fair young girl—tall, pale, sweet as an Easter lily—stood before her like an incarnate memory, pointing toward the past, the far-distant past, when she, too, was young, and pretty, and innocent, and gay—too pretty and too gay for a poor working girl! That was where the trouble began.

"I was light-haired, too," moaned old Marg, twisting her withered fingers restlessly. "Light-haired and light-complected! A pretty girl an' a good girl, too! Not like *her*. No! How could I be? Little the likes o' her knows what the likes o' me has to face!"

The bit of candle guttered and went out. The cold increased. It had ceased snowing, and a keen wind had arisen, tearing the clouds into shreds through which the stars gleamed. And presently the moon climbed up behind the belfry of the old church across the square and sent one broad white ray through the dingy window and across the floor. All at once the great bell began to strike the midnight hour, its mingled vibrations filling the garret with tumultuous sounds. The vision of the fair girl faded, and old Marg was herself again, a hard, bitter, rebellious old woman with a burning care where her heart had been, and only one thought, one desire, left in her desperate mind—the thought and the desire of death.

In young and passionate days she had often thought of seeking that way out of life's agonies, but at its worst there is always some sweetness left in the cup—when one is young! It was not so now. The dregs only had been hers for many a year, and she had had enough. Death—yes; that was best.

Her eyes glittered as she cast a look about the silent room. Bare, even of the means to this end! Ah, the window!

With an inarticulate cry the woman arose and hobbled along the shining moonray to the window and threw open the sash. Awed by the stern beauty of the heavens, the splendor of the moon tangled in the lace-like carvings of the belfry as in a net, she leaned some moments against the sill, looking out and down. Far below lay the deserted square, its white bosom traced with the sharp shadow of the tower. With a keen eye old Marg measured the distance, a sheer descent of 50 feet. Nothing to break the fall—nothing!

One movement, a swift fall, and that white surface would be broken by a black, shapeless heap. A policeman would find it on his next round, or some drunken reveler would stumble over it, or the good people on their way to early mass—ah! The seamed countenance lit up suddenly with a malignant joy.

But why not wait until they began to pass—those pious, respectable people in their comfortable furs and wools—and cast herself into their midst, a ghastly Christmas offering from Poverty to Riches, from Sin to Virtue? This suggestion commended itself highly to her sense of humor. With a hoarse chuckle she was about to close the window when a portion of the shadow that lay alongside the chimney showed signs of life, and rising on four long and skinny legs became a cat, a lean, black cat that crept meekly toward the window, its phosphorescent eyes gleaming, its lank jaws parted in a vain effort to mew. Startled, old Marg drew back for an instant. Then glancing from the animal to the pavement below, a brutal cunning, a malicious pleasure, lit up the witch-like features. Reaching out one skinny arm she called coaxingly, "Puss! Puss!"

The cat dragged herself up to the outstretched arm, rubbing her lank body caressingly against it.

The cruel, cunning old face softened suddenly. "Why!" muttered old Marg. "If she ain't a-tryin' to *purr!* Wall, that beats me!"

The poor beast continued its piteous appeal for aid, arching its starved frame, waving its tail, fawning unsuspectingly against the arm that had threatened.

With an impulse new to her misery-hardened heart, old Marg drew the animal in and closed the window. Far from resisting, the cat nestled against her with every sign of pleasure.

"She's been somebody's pet," said the old woman, placing her on the floor. "She ain't always been like this."

The divine emotion of pity, so new to this forlorn creature, grew and swelled in her bosom. The man at the hall had *not* lied, after all. Here was another of God's creatures as miserable as herself—nay, more so, for she had a roof to shelter her! And she could share it with this homeless one.

"Poor puss!" muttered old Marg, stroking the rough fur. "You're starvin', too, ain't ye? An' I ain't got nothin' to give ye, not a bite or a sip. Ah!"

Her eyes had fallen upon the discarded food. Eagerly, she seized it and placed it before the cat. The starving creature gnawed greedily at the bone an instant, then looked up with a hopeless mew. The old woman felt a keener pang of pity.

"Poor beast!" she said, with a bitter smile. "Ye can't eat 'em, can ye? No more could I! We're in the same box, puss! Old an' toothless an' nobody belongin' to us. We'll have to starve together, I guess. An' it's Christmas day! Did ye know that, puss? Christmas day! Dear! Dear!"

The cat rubbed against her skirts, her eyes fixed upon her benefactor's. "Seems to understand every word I say!" old Marg muttered. "If only I had a drop o' milk for her now!"

Hobbling to the stove, she examined the battered tin can, letting the moonlight shine into its rusty depths. A little water or tea remained in it, and with this she moistened some of the bread and placed it before the cat, who now devoured it eagerly. Then she took the animal in her arms and laid herself down on the mattress, drawing the ragged covers over them. The cat nestled against her side, the warmth of the two poor bodies mingling, and both slept.

The moonray crept along and spread itself over the heap of rags, the knotted fingers resting on the cat's rough fur, the seamed old face. It passed away, and morning dawned with a peal of bells and the sound of footsteps on the pavement below. And still the two slept on.

* * *

Angela stood near the door, receiving her Christmas guests. They came straggling in by twos and threes, some boldly and impudently, some shamefaced and shy, some eager, some indifferent, but all poverty-pinched. Each one was pleasantly welcomed and passed on to the feast. Angela watched and waited, and at last the door opened slowly to admit old Marg, who stopped short on the threshold with a look at once stubborn, appealing, suspicious, ashamed. Like a wild animal on the alert for the faintest sign of repulsion or danger, she stood there, but Angela only smiled, proffering her white, soft hand, destitute of jewels, but the hand of a lady.

"A Merry Christmas!" she said brightly.

"I was ugly to ye last night," said old Marg huskily, ignoring the beautiful hand she dared not touch.

"Never mind!" Angela answered sweetly. "You were tired."

"I am a bad old woman!" said old Marg, mistrustfully.

"Never mind that, either!" said Angela. "Let me be your friend. If you will, you shall never be cold or hungry again."

A profound wonder came into the old face. Then it began to writhe, and from each eye oozed scant tears, seeking a channel amid the seams and wrinkles of the sunken cheeks.

"You will let me be your friend," urged Angela.

Still old Marg wept silently, the scant tears of age.

"You shall have a pleasant home and—"

A swift, suspicious glance darted from the wet eyes. "Not a 'sylum, miss, please!" said the old woman.

"No," said Angela quietly. "Not an asylum. A home—a bright, clean, comfortable home—"

"I can work, miss!" put in old Marg, doubling her knotted hands to show their strength. "I can wash, an' scrub—"

"Yes," said Angela, "you may work all you are able, helping to keep things clean and comfortable."

Still old Marg looked doubtful. Wiping her cheeks with a corner of the shawl, she half turned toward the door.

"Have you a family, or anyone belonging to you?" asked Angela, thinking to have reached the root of the difficulty.

"Yes," said the old woman stoutly. "I have a cat. Where I go, she must go, too!"

Angela patted the grimy hand, and with a laugh that was good to hear she said, "I understand you perfectly. I have a cat of my own. You and *your* cat shall not be separated."

* * *

A half hour later entered the young man Robert. Angela pointed silently to old Marg sitting in a warm corner, contentedly munching her Christmas dinner.

"What have you done to her?" he asked. "She looks more human already."

Angela laughed again, that same laugh that goes to one's heart so. "I have adopted her—and her cat!" she answered. "That's all!"

Julia Schayer wrote for family and inspirational magazines late in the nineteenth century.

---

*A British board of fir or pine.

The Best Christmas Pageant Ever

Barbara Robinson

Thanks to those awful Herdman children no mother would permit her baby to be part of the annual Christmas pageant that year. Worse, none of the Herdmans knew anything about the Bible or the story of the Nativity. Yet here they were with the lead parts!

All over town unmitigated disaster was predicted.

Then came the long-anticipated night. . . .

Since the story and book first appeared in 1972, it has gone on to become one of the most beloved Christmas stories ever written.

The Herdmans moved from grade to grade through the Woodrow Wilson School like those South American fish that strip your bones clean in three minutes flat . . . which was just about what they did to one teacher after another.

I was always in the same grade with Imogene Herdman, and what I did was stay out of her way. As far as anyone could tell, Imogene was just like the rest of the Herdmans. She never learned anything, except dirty words and secrets about everybody.

It was no good trying to get secrets on the Herdmans. Everybody already knew about the awful things they did. They lied and stole and smoked cigars (even the girls). You couldn't even tease them about their parents, or holler, "Your father's in jail!" because they didn't care. Actually, they didn't know who their father was or where he was or anything about him, because when Gladys was 2 years old, he climbed on a railroad train and disappeared. Nobody blamed him. Mrs. Herdman worked double shifts at the shoe factory, and wasn't home much.

My mother's friend, Miss Philips, was a social service worker, and she tried to get some welfare money for the Herdmans so Mrs. Herdman could just work one shift and spend more time with her children. But Mrs. Herdman wouldn't do it; she liked the work, she said.

So the Herdmans pretty much looked after themselves. Ralph looked after Imogene, and Imogene looked after Leroy, and Leroy looked after Claude, and so on down the line. The big ones taught the little ones everything they knew . . . and the proof of that was that the meanest Herdman of all was Gladys, the youngest.

We figured they were headed straight for hell, by way of the state penitentiary . . . until they got themselves mixed up with the church, and my mother, and our Christmas pageant.

* * *

"We'll have our rehearsals on Wednesdays at 6:30," Mother said. "We're only going to have five rehearsals, so you must all try to be present at every one."

"What if we get sick?" asked a little kid in the front pew.

"You won't get sick," Mother told him, which was exactly what she told my little brother Charlie that morning when Charlie said he didn't want to be a shepherd and would be sick to his stomach if she made him be one.

"Now you little children in the cradle room and the primary class will be our angels," Mother said. "You'll like that, won't you?"

They all said yes. What else could they say?

"And we need Mary and Joseph, the three Wise Men, and the Angel of the Lord. I know that many of you would like to be Mary in our pageant, but, of course, we can have only one Mary. So I'll ask for volunteers, and then we'll all decide together which girl should get the part." That was pretty safe to say, since the only person who ever raised her hand was Alice Wendleken.

But Alice just sat there, chewing on a piece of her hair and looking down at the floor . . . and the only person who raised her hand this time was Imogene Herdman.

"Did you have a question, Imogene?" Mother asked. I guess that was the only reason she could think of for Imogene to have her hand up.

"No," Imogene said. "I want to be Mary." She looked back over her shoulder. "And Ralph wants to be Joseph."

"Yeh," Ralph said.

Mother just stared at them. It was like a detective movie when the nice little old gray-haired lady sticks a gun in the bank window and says "Give me all your money," and you can't believe it. Mother couldn't believe this.

"Well," she said after a minute, "we want to be sure that everyone has a chance. Does anyone else want to volunteer for Joseph?"

No one did.

"All right," Mother said, "Ralph will be our Joseph. Now, does anyone else want to volunteer for Mary?" Mother looked all around, trying to catch somebody's eye—*anybody's* eye. "Janet? . . . Roberta? . . . Alice, don't you want to volunteer this year?"

"No," Alice said, so low you could hardly hear her. Nobody volunteered to be Wise Men, either, except Leroy, Claude, and Ollie Herdman. So there was my mother, stuck with a Christmas pageant full of Herdmans in the main roles.

There was one Herdman left over, and one main role left over, and you didn't have to be very smart to figure out that Gladys was going to be the Angel of the Lord.

"What do I have to do?" Gladys wanted to know.

"The Angel of the Lord was the one who brought the good news to the shepherds," Mother said.

Right away all the shepherds began to wiggle around in their seats, figuring that any good news Gladys brought them would come with a smack in the teeth.

Charlie's friend, Hobie Carmichael, raised his hand and said, "I can't be a shepherd. We're going to Philadelphia."

"Why didn't you say so before?" Mother asked.

"I forgot."

One kid was honest. "Gladys Herdman hits too hard," he said.

"Why, Gladys isn't going to hit anybody!" Mother said. "What an idea! The Angel just visits the shepherds in the fields and tells them Jesus is born."

"And hits 'em," said the kid.

Of course, he was right. You could just picture Gladys whamming shepherds left and right, but Mother said that was perfectly ridiculous.

While everybody was leaving, Mother grabbed Alice Wendleken by the arm and said, "Alice, why in the world didn't you raise your hand to be Mary?"

"I don't know," Alice said, looking mad.

But I knew—I'd heard Imogene Herdman telling Alice what would happen to her if she dared to volunteer.

* * *

The first pageant rehearsal was usually about as much fun as a three-hour ride on the school bus, and just as noisy and crowded. This rehearsal, though, was different. Everybody shut up and settled down right away, for fear of missing something awful that the Herdmans might do.

They got there 10 minutes late, sliding into the room like a bunch of outlaws about to shoot up a saloon. Mother said, "And here's the Herdman family. We're glad to see you all," which was probably the biggest lie ever said right out loud in the church.

Mother separated everyone into angels and shepherds and guests at the inn, but right away she ran into trouble. The thing was, the Herdmans didn't know anything about the Christmas story. They knew that Christmas was Jesus' birthday, but everything else was news to them—the shepherds, the Wise Men, the star, the stable, the crowded inn.

It was hard to believe. At least, it was hard for me to believe—Alice Wendleken said she didn't have any trouble believing it.

"They never went to church in their whole life till your little brother told them we got refreshments," Alice said, "and all you ever hear about Christmas in school is how to make ornaments out of aluminum foil. So how would they know about the Christmas story?"

She was right. Of course, they might have read about it, but they never read anything except *Amazing Comics*. And they might have heard about it on TV, except that Ralph paid 65 cents for their TV at a garage sale, and you couldn't see anything on it unless somebody held on to the antenna.

The only other way for them to hear about the Christmas story was from their parents, and I guess Mr. Herdman never got around to it before he climbed on the railroad train. And it was pretty clear that Mrs. Herdman had given up ever trying to tell them anything.

* * *

Mother said she had better begin by reading the Christmas story from the Bible. This was a pain in the neck to most of us because we knew the whole thing backward and forward and never had to be told anything except who we were supposed to be, and where we were supposed to stand.

"*. . . Joseph and Mary, his espoused wife, being great with child . . .*"

"Pregnant!" yelled Ralph Herdman.

That stirred things up. All the big kids began to giggle, and all the little kids wanted to know what was so funny.

"I don't think it's very nice to say Mary was pregnant," Alice whispered to me.

"But she was," I pointed out.

Alice folded her hands in her lap and pinched her lips together. "I'd better tell my mother."

"Tell her what?"

"That your mother is talking about things like that in church. My mother might not want me to be here."

Among other things the Herdmans were famous for never sitting still and never paying attention to anyone—teachers, parents (their own or anybody else's), the truant officer, the police—yet here they were, eyes glued on my mother and taking in every word.

"What's that?" they would yell whenever they didn't understand the language, and when Mother read about there being no room at the inn, Imogene's jaw dropped and she sat up in her seat.

"Not even for Jesus?" she exclaimed.

"Well, now, after all," Mother explained, "nobody knew the baby was going to turn out to be Jesus."

"You said Mary knew," Ralph said. "Why didn't she tell them?"

"*I* would have told them!" Imogene put in. "Boy, would I have told them! What was the matter with Joseph that he didn't tell them? Her pregnant and everything," she grumbled.

"What was that they laid the baby in?" Leroy said. "That manger . . . is that like a bed? Why would they have a bed in the barn?"

"That's just the point," Mother said. "They *didn't* have a bed in the barn, so Mary and Joseph had to use whatever there was. What would you do if you had a new baby and no bed to put the baby in?"

"We put Gladys in a bureau drawer," Imogene volunteered.

"Well, there you are," Mother said, blinking a little.

"*Anyway,*" Mother continued, "Mary and Joseph used the manger. A manger is a large wooden feeding trough for animals."

"What were the wadded-up clothes?" Claude wanted to know.

"*Swaddling clothes,*" Mother sighed. "Long ago, people used to wrap their babies very tightly in big pieces of material, so they couldn't move around. It made the babies feel cozy and comfortable."

"You mean they tied him up and put him in a feedbox?" Gladys said. "Where was the Child Welfare?"

"'*And lo, the Angel of the Lord came upon them,*'" Mother went on, "'*and the glory of the Lord shone round about them, and—*'"

"Shazam!" Gladys yelled, flinging her arms out and smacking the kid next to her.

"What?" Mother said. Mother never read *Amazing Comics.*

"'*Now when Jesus was born in Bethlehem of Judea,*'" Mother went on reading, "'*behold there came Wise Men from the East to Jerusalem, saying—*'"

"What does it mean, Wise Men?" Ollie wanted to

know. "Were they like schoolteachers?"

"Actually, they were kings," Mother explained.

"Well, it's about time," Imogene muttered. "Maybe they'll tell the innkeeper where to get off, and get the baby out of the barn."

"'*They saw the young child with Mary, his mother, and fell down and worshiped him, and presented unto him gifts: gold and frankincense, and myrrh.*'"

"What's that stuff?" Leroy wanted to know.

"Precious oils," Mother said, "and fragrant resins."

"What kind of a cheap king hands out oil for a present? You get better presents from the firemen!"

Sometimes the Herdmans got Christmas presents at the Firemen's Party, but the Santa Claus always had to feel all around the packages to be sure they weren't getting bows and arrows or dart guns or anything like that.

Then we came to King Herod, and the Herdmans had never heard of him either, so Mother had to explain that it was Herod who sent the Wise Men to find the baby Jesus.

"Was it him that sent the crummy presents?" Ollie wanted to know, and Mother said it was worse than that—he planned to have the baby Jesus put to death.

"He just got born and already they're out to kill him?" Imogene asked.

The Herdmans wanted to know all about Herod, and I figured they liked him. He was so mean he could have been their ancestor—Herod Herdman. But I was wrong.

"Who's going to be Herod in this play?" Leroy said.

"We don't show Herod in our pageant," Mother said. And they all got mad. They wanted somebody to be Herod so they could beat up on him.

I couldn't understand the Herdmans. You would have thought the Christmas story came right out of the FBI files, they got so involved in it—wanted a bloody end to Herod, worried about Mary having her baby in a barn, and called the Wise Men a bunch of dirty spies.

And they left the first rehearsal arguing about whether Joseph should have set fire to the inn or just chased the innkeeper into the next county.

* * *

The next rehearsal Mother started, again, to separate everyone into angels and shepherds and guests at the inn, but she didn't get very far. The Herdmans wanted to rewrite the whole pageant and hang Herod for a finish.

Since none of the Herdmans had ever gone to church or Sunday school or read the Bible or anything, they didn't know how things were supposed to be. Imogene, for instance, didn't know that Mary was supposed to be acted out in one certain way—sort of quiet and dreamy and out of this world.

The way Imogene did it, Mary was a lot like Mrs. Santoro at the Pizza Parlor. "Get away from the baby!" she yelled at Ralph, who was Joseph. And she made the Wise Men keep their distance.

"The Wise Men want to honor the Christ Child," Mother explained for the tenth time. "They don't mean to harm him!"

But the Wise Men didn't know how things were supposed to be either, and nobody blamed Imogene for shoving them out of the way. You got the feeling that these Wise Men were going to hustle back to Herod as fast as they could and squeal on the baby, out of pure meanness.

They thought about it, too. "What if we *didn't* go home another way?" Leroy demanded. Leroy was Melchior. "What if we went back to the king and told on the baby—where he was and all?"

"He would murder Jesus," Ralph said. "Old Herod would murder him."

"I don't think it's very nice to talk about the baby Jesus being murdered," Alice said, stitching her lips together and looking sour. As we stood in the back row of the angel choir, Alice told me, "Be sure and tell your mother that I can step right in and be Mary if I have to. And if *I'm* Mary, we can get the Perkins baby for Jesus."

The way things stood, we didn't have any baby at all—and this really bothered my mother, because you couldn't very well have the best Christmas pageant in history with the chief character missing.

We had lots of babies offered in the beginning—until the mothers found out about the Herdmans. Mother had called everybody she knew, trying to rustle up a baby, but the closest she came was Bernice Watrous, who kept foster babies all the time.

"I've got a darling little boy right now," Bernice told Mother. "He's 3 months old, and so good I hardly know he's in the house. He'd be wonderful. Of course, he's Chinese. Does that matter?"

"No," Mother said. "It doesn't matter at all."

But Bernice's baby got adopted two weeks before Christmas, and Bernice said she didn't like to ask to borrow him back right away.

"We'll use a baby doll. That'll be better anyway," Mother said.

* * *

On the night of the pageant we didn't have any supper because Mother forgot to fix it. "When it's all over," my father said, "we'll go someplace and have hamburgers." But Mother said when it was all over she might want to go someplace and hide.

At 7:30 the pageant began. We sang two verses of *O Little Town of Bethlehem,* and then we were supposed to hum some more *O Little Town of Bethlehem* while Mary and Joseph came in from a side door. Only they didn't come right away. So we hummed and hummed and hummed, which is boring and also very hard, and before long doesn't sound like any song at all—more like an old refrigerator.

"I knew something like this would happen," Alice Wendleken whispered to me. "They didn't come at all! We won't have any Mary and Joseph—and now what are we supposed to do?"

I guess we would have gone on humming till we all turned blue, but we didn't have to. Ralph and Imogene were there all right, only for once they didn't come through the door pushing each other out of the way. They just stood there for a minute as if they weren't sure they were in the right place—because of the candles, I guess, and the church being full of people. They looked like the people you see on the 6:00 news—refugees.

It suddenly occurred to me that this was just the way it must have been for the real Holy Family, stuck away in a barn by people who didn't much care what

77

happened to them. They couldn't have been very neat and tidy either, but more like *this* Mary and Joseph (Imogene's veil was cockeyed as usual, and Ralph's hair stuck out all around his ears). Imogene had the baby doll, but she wasn't carrying it the way she was supposed to, cradled in her arms. She had it slung up over her shoulder, and before she put it in the manger, she thumped it twice on the back.

I heard Alice gasp and she poked me. "I don't think it's very nice to burp the baby Jesus," she whispered, "as if he had colic."

Right away we had to sing *While Shepherds Watched Their Flocks by Night*—and we had to sing very loud, because there were more shepherds than there were anything else, and they made so much noise, banging their crooks around like a lot of hockey sticks.

Next came Gladys, from behind the angel choir, pushing people out of the way and stepping on everyone's feet. Since Gladys was the only one in the pageant who had anything to say she made the most of it: "Hey! Unto you a child is born!" she hollered, as if it was, for sure, the best news in the world. And all the shepherds trembled, afraid of Gladys, mainly, but it looked good anyway.

We got a little rest then, while the boys sang *We Three Kings of Orient Are* and everybody in the audience shifted around to watch the Wise Men march up the aisle.

"What have they got?" Alice whispered.

I didn't know, but whatever it was, it was heavy— Leroy almost dropped it. He didn't have his frankincense jar either, and Claude and Ollie didn't have anything, although they were supposed to bring the gold and the myrrh.

"I knew this would happen," Alice said for the second time. "I bet it's something awful."

It was a ham—and right away I knew where it came from. My father was on the church charitable works committee—they give away food baskets at Christmas, and this was the Herdmans' food basket ham. It still had the ribbon around it saying Merry Christmas.

"I'll bet they stole that!" Alice said.

"They did not. And if they want to give away their own ham, I guess they can do it." But even if the Herdmans didn't like ham (that was Alice's next idea), they had never before in their lives given anything away except lumps on the head. So you had to be impressed.

Leroy dropped the ham in front of the manger, and they went and sat down in the only space that was left.

While we sang *What Child Is This?* the Wise Men were supposed to confer among themselves and then leave by a different door so everyone would understand that they were going home another way. But the Herdmans forgot, or didn't want to, or something, because they didn't confer and they didn't leave, either. They just sat there, and there wasn't anything anyone could do about it.

"They're ruining the whole thing!" Alice whispered, but they weren't at all. As a matter of fact, it made perfect sense for the Wise Men to sit down and rest, and I said so.

"They're supposed to have come a long way. You wouldn't expect them just to show up, hand over the ham, and leave!"

As for ruining the whole thing, it seemed to me

that the Herdmans had improved the pageant a lot, just by doing what came naturally—like burping the baby, for instance, or thinking a ham would make a better present than a lot of perfumed oil.

Everyone had been waiting all this time for the Herdmans to do something absolutely unexpected. And sure enough, that was what happened.

Imogene Herdman was crying. In the candlelight her face was all shiny with tears, and she didn't even bother to wipe them away. She just sat there—awful old Imogene, in her crookedy veil—crying and crying and crying.

* * *

Well. It was the best Christmas pageant we ever had. Everybody said so, but nobody seemed to know why. When it was over, people stood around the lobby of the church, talking about what was different this year. There was something special, everyone said—but they couldn't put their finger on what.

And this was the funny thing about it all. For years I'd thought about the wonder of Christmas, and the mystery of Jesus' birth, and never really understood it. But now, because of the Herdmans, it didn't seem so mysterious after all.

When we came out of the church that night it was cold and clear, with crunchy snow underfoot and bright, bright stars overhead. And I thought about the Angel of the Lord—Gladys, with her skinny legs and her dirty sneakers sticking out from under her robe, yelling at all of us, everywhere: *"Hey! Unto you a child is born!"*

Barbara Robinson, a prolific author, lives and writes in Pennsylvania. Because of this story, she has become a household name in North America.

One to Cherish

Lucy Parr

The year was almost over and the Christmas cards must be written on and sent. But what could she write? So little of significance had happened to her family.

That's it—maybe they'd help her!

As she passed the table, Amy Barton ran her hand across the top box of Christmas cards, as she had a number of times in the past few days.

I must *get those letters started*, she thought. She went on to the other tasks that must be completed in the too short time that remained before Christmas, but her mind stayed with the letters. What was there to write about? Nothing earthshaking had happened to the Bartons. The year was old and tired, made up of bits and scraps and snippets. How did one weave an interesting account from that?

Amy hurried dinner preparations. The idea bloomed when the family was gathered around the table. "We'll start with Daddy," she said. "Then from Betsy down to Kendall." She laughed self-consciously as all eyes turned to her. "It's sort of a game. I want each of you to tell the one thing you remember best from this year. Happy or sad, good or bad. Something you think stands out from the year."

It was a slightly sneaky way of getting help in jogging her memory, but perhaps she had forgotten some newsworthy items.

Don tipped his head a little as he always did when thinking deeply. And when he spoke, it was with surprising seriousness. "The best memory? It's been having you get breakfast for me at 6:15 every workday morning this entire year. Even when you were miserable with the flu you'd refuse to sleep in. And not once did you indicate that to do so was a 'duty.' I've heard the other men at work. Breakfast—at home—for a husband has gone out of style."

Amy smiled shakily. This wasn't quite what she had expected when she made her request, but nice. She had thought of it as such a small contribution when Don worked so hard for all of them.

The children had already turned toward Betsy, waiting for her one best thing. Without hesitation she said, "My dress—for graduation. It was only for junior high, yet you spent all of that time making it. It made me feel almost like a—a princess, the way I used to when I was little. But even more important," Betsy added, "was that all of you were there to see me graduate. A lot of the parents didn't think it was important enough for changing plans. Debbie's mother wouldn't even give up a bridge game, when she plays bridge twice every week."

Betsy's words brought the memory back to Amy. Betsy *had* looked like a princess beside many of the girls who tried to look mature beyond their years.

Ryan began to speak hesitantly, in starts and stops, as if finding his way through unfamiliar emotions. "The thing that stays sharpest—for me . . . It's funny, I guess . . ." He took a swallow of milk. "Well, you know—you remember in August. When that bunch of guys went to Hank Jamison's station that night"—Amy glanced quickly at Don—"well, you know, the way the guys broke into the station and messed the place up with all that oil and grease. Because Hank was a straight talker when they tried hanging around the station and goofing off and all."

Ryan paused for another gulp of milk. And Amy's heart turned over as it had when she first heard of the vandalism, knowing that Ryan had requested to go out with the fellows that evening.

"Well, I guess Joe Elton would have known where to look for the guys who were responsible—even if he hadn't gone by in his patrol car just as they were sneaking out the back door." Ryan looked at his father and swallowed convulsively before he went on.

"The guys hadn't planned anything like that, Mike Weeks told me. Only to tear open the cases of oil and put the cans in crazy places all over the station. Not to open the cans—or anything like that. But you know how something like that can grow, if one guy starts daring another."

"I know, son, I know," Don said. "I've been in that spot."

"Sure—sure you have. And I guess that's why you wouldn't let me go with the guys. I guess you know I was mad when you wouldn't let me go. I didn't have a good answer about where the guys were going—didn't know what they had in mind."

The words rushed on. "Most of all, I remember now

that you *cared* enough not to let me go. Even when I acted like a sorehead and said some hard things. But now I haven't been in trouble with the law the way the other guys have. That isn't going to follow me wherever I go. And it doesn't hang over you and Mom."

Ryan's best memory . . . a nonhappening, but so fine.

"My best memory . . ." It was 10-year-old Lisa. "My best memory was last summer, when we went camping at Twin Lakes. That was the very best vacation we ever did have. The whole time. Even if there hadn't been that last day, when I almost beat Daddy and the big kids swimming across the lake."

It had been a good vacation, Amy remembered. And to think Don had been upset because there hadn't been money for a *real* vacation this year. He'd been disappointed that they'd had to settle for a few days of tenting in the mountains only 25 miles from home.

Kendall was only 4. What could he remember of the year? He glanced around the table, enjoying his moment of being the center of attention.

"The best thing of all—the very best thing"–the little "ham" paused for effect, then the words whistled out—"the very best thing is that we have love at *our* house. Even when someone little ["someone little" always meant himself] does something naughty and has to be scolded and spanked. Like even when someone little broke Mama's pretty vase—even after Mama told him to stop roughing in the house—even when she cried she didn't get all mean and shouty the way some mothers get over teeny little things."

Amy smiled. She was thinking how near she had come to shrieking about the vase. She was glad that she had held back. That they had preserved love at their house so that a 4-year-old would notice.

She hadn't expected the responses she had received to her game. Perhaps—if one wove together all of the bright bits and scraps and snippets . . .

"*You* didn't say yet, Mama," Kendall broke into her thoughts. "You didn't say what was best."

"Sure, Mom," Ryan insisted. "You say, too."

Amy's voice came out with a breathless sound. "Why, for me, it's been the entire year—a good year."

Later, when she sat down to begin the letters, that was what she said:

"Dear Aunt Ruth, This has been a good year for the Bartons. One to cherish . . ."

Lucy Parr wrote for family magazines during the second half of the twentieth century.

The Easter Christmas Tree

Arlene Anibal, as told to Marilyn Tworog

It was Christmas, but there was no money to buy any-
thing. Hardly anything to eat but a leftover piece of candy
from a box given last Easter. It was truly a dismal Christmas
until . . .

*T*he dazzling lights on the Christmas tree made sparkles
on my daughter's hair—light and dark, light and dark.
Candle glow and firelight warmed her face as she sat at my
knee on the cricket stool. She could have been 5 instead of 30,
this only girl child, our youngest. I reached out to touch her
dark, honey hair just as she turned her face upward and said,
"Mama, tell me a story about when you were a little girl."

An Ohio winter wind blew through my memory,
and I could feel the damp chill of Christmas 1924. I was
7 years old and hungry. Father had been a railroad man.
We were never rich, but we had plenty of love.

Four years before, my railroader father had been killed
on the tracks near our home. My two older brothers and
sister had had to leave home to find work in the city.

Mother and I were left alone on the farm—no

income, not much food, our nearest neighbor two miles
away. Roy and Arthur and Dorothy sent what little
they could spare from their tiny incomes as hotel dishwasher, busboy, and drugstore clerk. We didn't have
much of anything, Mother and I, just each other.

The day before Christmas Mother and I sat down
for a special holiday treat—one chocolate candy,
shared. One of my sister's more affluent boyfriends had
given Mother and me a five-pound box of chocolates
for Easter. We had made them last till now.

"Just one, honey. See how long you can make it
last."

As I cautiously picked the last creamy candy from
its fluted holder, I felt the holiday spirit filling my heart
with joy. A special day was coming—we were sharing
the last piece of candy. Mother cut it in half with the
kitchen knife, and we silently dissolved our treat.

Today the candy was our lunch. Other days Mother
had crushed up a piece or two and spread the mixture on
bread. A chocolate sandwich was a treat to me. I didn't
understand my Mother's silence as we solemnly took
slow bites of "dinner." I didn't see her tears the day she
carefully calculated that if we ate just one handful of
cornmeal made into mush each day the yellow meal
would last through the winter till the tax money arrived.

But Christmas was coming! I'd been hungry before,
so I wouldn't miss a big Christmas dinner. And there
never were very many presents.

I felt like Christmas inside, but the house looked
just as bare and empty as ever. My sister had told me
stories of how the city looked at Christmas, but I had
never seen a "Christmasy" city, so it was hard for me to

visualize this scene in my childish mind.

I did remember other more prosperous Christmases in our home, however, and I felt the absence of that warm, happy, festive feeling when our family had been together and there had been carefully guarded whisperings and secret sharing looks on Christmas Eve. This is what our bare farm kitchen lacked that memorable year.

As I ate my candy ever so slowly and thought and wondered about Christmas, I didn't see my mother's eyes sadly sweeping the bleak room. The next thing I knew, Mother reached for my hand in an unexpected gesture of affection and said, "Honey, let's go get us a Christmas tree." I was awed to silence by the surprise and joy of this unfamiliar togetherness with Mother, whose hard and troubled life had erased her happiness.

Hand in hand, we walked out into the damp Ohio air of winter. We went by the woodshed, and Mother picked up an axe. I couldn't help giving a little hop of excitement. (Hopping also made me warmer.) My thin coat did little to keep out the snow-flecked wind. But a Christmas light was glowing brighter and brighter inside me.

We walked among the trees for a long time. I prolonged the finding of a tree as an excuse to cling to Mother's hard, calloused hand. We searched and searched, but the evergreen trees were all too big. I noticed a look of silent despair creep over my mother's face.

I took advantage of the occasion and bravely squeezed her hand. "Don't worry, Mama, we'll find a tree."

She smiled down at me. "Sure we will, honey. There's a Christmas tree out in these woods somewhere."

"Oh, Mama, look!" I pointed to a leafless little tree about two feet high. "That's a pretty tree, and just the right size!"

My mother looked at the bare spiky limbs, and thoughts of other Christmases brought the sting of tears to her eyes. But what else was there this year? She forced her cold lips into a smile and almost reluctantly, I thought, let go of my hand to chop down the tree.

Lighthearted, I skipped beside her through the

snowy trees back to the farmhouse. We shook the snow off our coats and rubbed our hands warm at the wood stove. Then with the utmost care we propped up the bare branchy tree on the kitchen table and stood back to admire "our tree." I danced around the table and clapped my hands with delight. "A real tree for Christmas, Mama! Is it Christmas now?"

"Not quite, honey, we have to decorate our tree first."

I wondered what that would mean since tree ornaments were nonexistent at our house. But then I saw Mother reach for the empty candy box, and a vision of possible beauty came to my young mind. "Oh, we do have decorations, don't we, Mama?"

Mother just smiled as she dismantled the candy box. The green waxy paper that divided the rows of candy wound as if by magic around the bare branches of the tree. Together we smoothed every scrap of gold, silver, green, and red foil that had once held Easter candy. And carefully Mother molded the bits around shells of walnuts and buckeyes as I leaned, elbows on table, to watch her closely. And suddenly we had a green tree with ornaments! I jumped up and down with excitement, and Mother smiled in her quiet way.

"Want to pop some corn to string on it?" she asked.

To spend so much happy time with Mother was almost more "Christmas" than I could take all at once. We threaded the puffy popcorn in long strands, and Mother looped it with artistry on the bare twigs. Then she lit the oil lamp, put it on the table by the tree, and we sat together in the rocking chair on Christmas Eve.

I don't remember anything special for Christmas dinner the next day. Perhaps Mother had miraculously managed to save back ingredients to make a small gingerbread for the two of us as she had previously done for very special occasions. The other children couldn't come home, and I don't recall if my sister, Dorothy, or the boys sent presents. But I do remember the Easter Christmas tree and the togetherness and the love we shared that day.

I look beyond my daughter's head resting on my lap to our beautifully decorated Christmas tree. Blue glass balls, blue velvet ribbons, gold and white lights winking on and off. Embers glowing in the brick fireplace. Mantovani bringing a holiday orchestra to our home. Gifts piled high beneath the tree—boxes wrapped with taste and elegance and love.

As I harbor secrets of what some of those boxes contain— gifts for my own daughter—I think I at last understand how Mama must have felt that Christmas Eve as she looked through misty eyes at her little girl's sunny blonde hair in the lamplight and had to dismiss all that she would liked to have done.

I long to tell her that of all the many beautiful Christmas Eves we had in the following years, the only one I really remember was the Easter Christmas tree. I was a happy little girl, made so by the love that prompted Mother to do what she could for me. And as I stroke my girl's hair, warm with firelight, I remember Christmas 1924 and feel the warmth of sacrifice.

Arlene Anibal and Marilyn Tworog wrote for inspirational magazines during the second half of the twentieth century.

The Christmas Stocking

Julie Rae Rickard

He was a 9-year-old that long ago Christmas, and already well on his way toward becoming a cynic. But barring the way to that condition was a thing called "extra credit" and a girl named Carol.

There is something truly magical about Christmas Eve. For just a few hours the world seems to stand still, as if holding its breath for the miracle.

My favorite, most magical Christmas Eve was more than 20 years ago. It seems like only yesterday that I was an anxious little boy, tossing and turning in bed, waiting for morning to arrive. That same year I learned the truth about Santa and was in danger of losing my Christmas spirit forever. I know my parents meant well, but I was disappointed in them. They had lied to me. If it were not for Carol, I think I would have become a cynic at 9 years of age. Sometimes it's ironic how things work out. Just when you are about to lose faith, it comes looking for you.

* * *

It was the fall of 1973 when our teacher, Mrs. Johnson, asked if anyone wanted to volunteer to help the Salvation Army in exchange for extra credit in social studies. I quickly raised my hand. Helping the poor would really impress Mom and Grandma, and I knew Santa would like it.

I first saw Carol in the back room of the Salvation Army building. She smiled when we were introduced and shook my hand. "Nice to meet you, Matt." In a few minutes she had me sorting canned goods. She had such a nice laugh that it made me feel good to hear it. I liked being around her, yet something about her gave me a funny feeling in my stomach. The next week I volunteered again.

My heart skipped a beat when I learned I would be working with Carol again. This time we were sorting out donated clothing. I rushed up to her. "Hi, Carol!"

"Hello, Matt." She smiled as she dropped some winter scarves into a box. "It's good to see you back. Most of the boys only come here once."

"Why is that?" I asked cautiously as she handed me a garbage bag full of clothes.

She shrugged. "I don't know. Most only come if it gives them extra credit in school."

I swallowed hard and guiltily stared into the bag.

"Isn't that why you are here?"

"No!" I quickly looked up to see her shaking her head.

"My pastor said everyone should try to help where and whenever they can, and I believe that, too."

"Oh, yeah. Me too." I buried my head in the bag and shuffled through the clothes as if I knew what I was doing.

I must have looked guilty because soon she was laughing. Slowly I looked up. She had her hand over her mouth. "What?" I asked.

She smiled. "You're here for extra credit, aren't you?"

"Yeah," I muttered without looking up. Then I felt her hand on my shoulder.

"It's OK, Matt," she said in a wonderfully silky voice. "We all have to start somewhere."

After that I started going to the Salvation Army on my own, without Mrs. Johnson. I wasn't doing it to impress anyone, not my mother, grandmother, or even Santa. I wanted to see Carol.

Little by little, I learned more about her. She was 11, older than she looked. She came from the other side of town, where the poorer families lived. There were five kids in her family, and she shared a bedroom with two sisters. She had only three different outfits. Part of me wanted to feel sorry for her, yet she seemed so much happier than I did.

As it got closer to Christmas, I asked a stupid question. "What is Santa bringing you?"

She started to speak and then stopped, hesitating for more than a minute before saying, "What I'd really like to get for Christmas is a telescope."

"Telescope?" It seemed like such an "un-girl" thing to want.

"Yes." She laid the coat down on the

table in front of her and brushed it off. "I want to be an astronomer. What do you want, Matt?" she asked as she turned to hang the coat up with the others.

"Well, I really want that smash-'em-up car set, a football uniform, some matchbox cars, one of those new super-duper squirt rifles, and some new cars for my train set." I looked at her, and her mouth was hanging slightly open in shock.

"How many of these things do you think you are going to get?" she asked, puzzled.

"Why, all of them. I've been really good. Santa will bring most of it. Of course, Mom and Dad will get me things. And Grandma and my Uncle Nick and—" I stopped, suddenly realizing that I was listing more presents than she ever received on a Christmas morning. But why wouldn't Santa bring her what she wanted?

She shook her head. "I'll be lucky to get my telescope."

I had to ask. "Why do you think Santa won't get you a telescope?"

She smiled slightly, turning away from me. "Maybe I'm not as good as you think." She hung up another coat.

Carol not good? How could that be? Maybe she was working in the Salvation Army because she was some kind of juvenile delinquent. "Did you do something bad?" I whispered as I leaned forward.

She laughed out loud, startling me. I jumped back. "No, no, no." She shook her head and turned back to me. There were tears in her eyes, but she was smiling. "I'm getting too old for Santa."

Just then someone yelled that my mother was outside, waiting to pick me up. I quickly said goodbye to Carol, and

on the way home I told my mother I wanted a telescope.

That night as I was trying to get to sleep, I thought a lot about Santa. The Salvation Army was collecting toys for poor kids. Carol and I worked together, separating toys and matching them up to the lists the kids made. Why were the kids giving their lists to the Salvation Army instead of to Santa? It didn't make any sense—unless there was no Santa!

I got out of bed and sat at the window, leaning my elbows on the windowsill, my chin resting in my palms. The night was clear and the stars shone brightly over the light dusting of snow. No Santa. No special man who can make your dreams come true. Only Mom, Dad, and Sears.

I jumped up and ran out of my room, determined to ask my parents about this Santa conspiracy. From the hallway I could hear the TV. I slowly started down the stairs, hesitating when I heard them talking about me.

"A telescope?" my father was saying. "Where did he get that idea?"

"I don't know," my mother answered. "Do you know where I can get one?"

"I'm sure there are some in the Sears catalog," he replied. "Now, do we want this to be from us, or from Santa?"

The truth was out—there was no real Santa. I felt stupid for believing. And to make matters worse, Carol knew I was stupid enough to believe. No wonder she laughed at me.

It was the week before Christmas, and I was supposed to go with Carol and one of the adult volunteers to ring the bell and collect money outside the mall. I told my mother I was sick and couldn't go. Truth was, I couldn't face Carol. I felt so stupid.

I was lying in bed thinking how I'd never feel that magic of Christmas Eve again when Mom knocked on my door to say there was someone to see me. When I got downstairs, there was Carol, waiting at the door.

"I hope you're feeling better, Matt," she said. "I wanted to see if you'd change your mind about coming with us tonight. Mrs. Wilson is waiting in the car outside."

When I didn't answer she said, "If you don't come, I will be stuck alone with her. You know how stuffy she is. I won't have any fun if you don't come."

How could I refuse those eyes?

Then Mom spoke up. "Oh, Matty, look at your hair!" She fussed with it, and I felt 4 years old.

"Mom!" I said, pushing her away. To my relief, Carol seemed oblivious to this. "I do feel better," I told her.

"Are you sure, Matt?" Mom asked. "You still look pale." She put her palm on my forehead. "Do you have a fever?"

"Mom," I protested, "I'm OK. Can I go?"

She looked from me to Carol, who was trying not to laugh. "OK, but if you start to feel sick . . ."

I was already running up to my room.

When we got to the mall it was snowing a little. Mrs. Wilson said it was too cold for her to stand outside, so she went into the mall to warm up. Carol was ringing the bell and thanking those who stopped to deposit their change in our bucket. Her cheeks were as red as the bucket from the cold, but she was beautiful.

"Why didn't you want to come tonight? Is it me?" she asked softly as if she didn't want anyone else to hear.

I looked up at her in shock. "No. Why would it be you?"

She frowned, then took her hands out of her pockets and blew on them. "I thought maybe I offended you the other day." She rubbed her hands together and looked away.

"When?"

A man in an expensive coat dropped $5 into the bucket.

"Thank you!" Carol said to him with a big smile. As he walked away she looked at me again. "When we talked about Santa. I'm sorry if you thought Santa wasn't coming to see you. I know he will." She looked down and shuffled her feet. I realized they were cold and her boots were well worn.

"I've been thinking a lot and, well, I guess I don't believe in Santa anymore," I said. I told her about overhearing my parents and that I was disappointed in them. I was upset that there was no magic in Christmas.

To my surprise, she laughed. "Matt, does your family go to church?"

"Yes, on Christmas and Easter."

She nodded. "What do you know about the original Christmas story?"

"Mary. Joseph. The inn. Baby Jesus. The Wise Men."

"Matt, that is the true magic of Christmas. God sent us His Son as the ultimate gift. His Son taught us all we need to know about love and living."

To be honest, I hadn't thought much about the Jesus story. It was just a story they told at church. My family wasn't religious. We never talked about Jesus or God. I knew Christmas was Jesus' birthday, but that's as far as it went.

"Matt," Carol said, looking at me intently, "to discover the true magic of Christmas you need to believe in Jesus, not Santa."

Mrs. Wilson came back then, and we asked if we could go into the mall and get warm. She reluctantly agreed and feebly began ringing the bell.

Carol and I slipped inside the mall where she told me all about Jesus and His miracles. As we walked past the mall Santa, I looked at the eager faces of the children waiting to see the man in the red suit. I wanted to tell them all it was a lie.

"Don't be so bitter, Matt," she warned. "People have a right to believe what they want. Sometimes people have to be disappointed in something before they find what they really need."

Sensing my unhappiness, she changed the subject, "What was your best Christmas ever?" When I didn't answer, she continued, "All my Christmases are special. My brothers and sisters and I get up early to exchange the gifts we make for each other. We always make each other things. Did I tell you that before?" She hesitated a minute. "No, I probably didn't because I didn't want you to know how poor we are. Anyway, we draw or sew something for each other. Last year I made a cloth football for my younger brother. It wasn't quite like a real football, but he really liked it. We played with it for a few months before it fell apart."

She led me over to a bench and we sat down. The red in her cheeks was fading, and she stopped blowing on her hands. She was excited as she spoke about her family. "After we open each other's gifts we open what our parents gave us. We each get only one gift. Sometime it's only a shirt or dress."

I was really feeling sorry for her. She truly came from a different world.

"Then we all go down to the hall where the Salvation Army serves its Christmas dinner. I know it may sound like a depressing way to spend Christmas, but my family likes to volunteer to serve that day."

"Oh, your family is *serving*."

"Yes," she answered. "We don't have to go there. Though there have been years that we haven't had a meal at home ourselves. But usually in the evening we go home for our family Christmas dinner."

"Is this why you volunteer so much? Because they help your family?"

"No, because they help every family. And if you come down on Christmas Day I'll show you why it's the best way to spend Christmas."

What would Mom and Dad say? Our Christmas morning was filled with presents. And then we always went to Grandma's for dinner and to open more presents. It was the one day, other than my birthday, that the family really spent time with me. "I'll have to ask my mother," I answered.

"Tell your parents to come, too," she said innocently.

"I will," I answered with little hope.

Mrs. Wilson was waving to us and shivering, so we hurried back to our posts.

* * *

On Christmas Eve I was depressed.

"You'll have to get to bed early tonight," Mom said. "You don't want Santa to see you up past your bedtime."

I nodded. It was only 6:30. I thought about what Carol and her family were doing. She said on Christmas Eve they sang Christmas songs. That sounded like fun. On the surface it seemed that my family had everything. But the truth was, Carol's family was the one who had everything they needed. They had the things that mattered most—faith, hope and love.

It wasn't that my parents didn't love me. They were just too busy to really spend time with me. Mom had all her social affairs, and Dad was always working late. I envied Carol whose parents were never too busy to talk to her. She was close to her brothers and sisters.

Suddenly I wanted to see Carol. I still hadn't given her the small present I had bought with the last of my allowance. I really wanted to give it to her tonight. So I asked my mother if we could go to Carol's and drop off the gift. In the spirit of Christmas, she actually agreed, as long as she didn't have to go into their house.

She drove me to Carol's in silence. As we pulled into the driveway, I could see the lights of their little tree reflected on the snow outside.

"Don't be too long," Mom said as I slipped out of the car.

I hurried to the door and knocked. I could hear singing inside—"Away in a Manger." I knocked again before the singing stopped and a woman opened the door.

"Hello," she said softly in a voice much like Carol's. Her eyes widened when she saw my mother's car. "You must be Matt!" she said before turning and calling for Carol. "Come on in. She'll be right here." She gestured, and I stepped into Carol's world.

The small house seemed even tinier inside, but it was warm. I saw eyes like Carol's peering at me through several different faces, all smiling and happy. Carol stepped away from the others and came toward me.

"Matt! How nice of you to come. Look, everyone, this is Matt!"

"Hi, Matt," they said, almost in unison.

I smiled and felt bad for not bringing each of them a gift. There were only a few packages under their tree.

"Can you stay?" she asked hopefully.

"No. Mom is waiting." I looked down into my gloved hands at the little present. "I just wanted to give you this and say Merry Christmas." I held it out to her.

She smiled. "Oh, Matt, you didn't have to. But I have something for you, too."

She set my present on the table that was covered with Christmas cookies—homemade ones, not like the ones Mom bought at the store. She reached into the cabinet and pulled out a small package of her own. It was wrapped in newspaper. She handed it to me. "Open mine first," she encouraged.

I nodded and slowly opened the paper. It was a Christmas stocking with my name embroidered on the top.

"I made it myself," she said proudly. "Look inside."

I reached into the stocking and found a few football cards, a small plastic kaleidoscope, and a little Bible. When I looked up at her, she was beaming. "Do you like it?"

She had made it herself. The edges weren't quite even and the material wasn't new. Yet it was the most beautiful thing I had ever seen.

Mom beeped the horn, startling me, prodding me to finally answer, "Yes, very much." Carol was the sweetest person I ever knew. "Open yours."

"OK!" Slowly, she slipped the paper off. She pulled out a new pair of gloves from the box and put them on. They just fit. "Thank you! Oh, Matt. This is wonderful." She hugged me.

I didn't know what to do. "I bought them myself, with my own money," I said, trying to make the gift sound more special.

"Matt, that is so sweet," her mother said, and suddenly I remembered that we weren't alone. Her whole family was now around us, admiring the gloves.

Then Mom beeped the horn again. "I have to go," I explained. "Have a Merry Christmas."

Mom was slightly irritated. "How poor are they?" she asked when I got in the car. "That house is a shambles. How can anyone live there? Poor girl! We probably should have gotten her something more. I noticed she could use a new coat and boots and—"

I tuned her out as she listed all the things we could do to "help" Carol's family. Mother didn't seem to understand that having more "things" was not the answer.

"What is that?" she asked as she finally noticed the little stocking. "Is that what she gave you?"

"She made it herself." I looked down at it again. It was so imperfect, yet perfect.

Later, in the darkness of my room, I held onto the stocking. No one had ever made anything for me before. It must have taken her a lot of time to sew it. I turned on the light to look at it again. I looked at it through the kaleidoscope. Then I started to read the Bible. It was the first Christmas Eve that I wasn't waiting for Santa. But because of Carol, there was still magic.

The next morning I opened my gifts. Funny how now it seemed more of a chore than fun. There was the smash-em-up car set, the matchbox cars, a train set, the football outfit, and, of course, the telescope and a few dozen other things. None of the gifts gave me the pleasure I felt when Carol had opened her present and saw the gloves. Maybe there was something to this "it's-better-to-give-than-to-receive" stuff.

We went to Grandma's, which was also on the other side of town but across the tracks. I realized on the way that it would be a short walk to the fire hall, where the Salvation Army was serving their meal. After dinner, when everyone was drowsy, I slipped out and walked down to the fire hall. I opened the door slowly and saw people smiling, heard people laughing and then singing again.

"Matt!" I turned to see Carol rushing toward me. She was wearing a Christmas apron. "It's so good to see you here!"

I felt all warm inside. "Did you have a good Christmas?" I asked.

She seemed puzzled at my meaning. "It's not over yet."

"I mean, did you get what you wanted this morning?"

"I got everything I needed," she said and looked away.

She was still missing the point. "Did you get a telescope?"

She hung her head. "No. Dad said he tried, but he couldn't find one he could afford. But I got new boots!" She smiled and pointed to her feet. "Come on in!" She pulled me into the crowd. "Did you eat? Do you need anything?" Then she seemed to realize it was a silly question. "What would you like to do?"

What I really wanted was to follow her anywhere, to steal some of her Christmas spirit.

As she led me around, the kids beamed as they showed me the toys the Salvation Army had provided for them. I felt guilty that there were more toys under my tree than there were in this whole building. We sang Christmas songs, talked, and joked.

Then a young girl came in with her family and I learned what sharing is really about. They were obviously very poor, and some of the workers helped them to feel comfortable as Carol's mother served them dinner. Other helpers saw to it that each child had a gift to open. I smiled as I watched the kids' excitement.

Carol was talking to a girl who was about her own age, but they were too far away for me to hear them. After a few minutes Carol's smile disappeared and she waved to me to join her.

"What's wrong?"

"Would you walk me back to my house for a moment? I have to pick something up."

"OK," I agreed. "But I need to get back to my grandma's soon."

We walked briskly to her house. She ran inside and came out with a box. It took me a few minutes to realize what she had done. She had changed out of her new boots and put on her old ones.

"Where are your new boots?" I asked as we ran.

"In the box."

"Why are they in the box?"

"I'm giving them to that girl who just came in."

"What? Why are you giving your new boots away?"

"I have boots that serve me just fine. She has no boots at all. Her feet are all wet. She will get sick if she doesn't have boots."

I was shocked as she gave her new boots to a stranger. What planet was this girl and her family from? No one was *that* nice. But as evening came I saw that Carol and her family were genuinely sincere in their giving. They believed God would care for them, no matter what. They had faith that all they had was all they needed. If they needed anything more, God would provide it for them. They felt no need to hold on to material things. As I walked back to my grandmother's house I knew I would never be the same.

A few days later the Salvation Army had a thank-you party for all the people who had helped during the season. I didn't have a problem getting my mother to take me there, but she didn't understand why I was taking bags of toys. I explained it by saying that I wanted to show them my new things.

Carol was shocked when she saw me carrying so many bags. "Who do you think you are—Santa?" she joked.

"Yes," I smiled. "I'm donating all these toys."

Carol smiled. "Are you sure you are only 9? You suddenly seem to be grown up."

Embarrassed, I looked down. "I have something for you." I led her into the entryway and pointed to the bag I'd left there.

She smiled awkwardly. "You didn't have to get me anything else."

"Yes, I did. Look inside."

"Really, Matt. You shouldn't."

She was embarrassed. Embarrassed that I was rich and

she was poor. Well, she had shared her wealth with me, and now it was time to share mine with her.

"Carol, it's OK. God told me you needed these."

She was unable to argue with that and reached in the bag. "A new pair of boots? Matt, I don't know what to say." She hugged me, and I was glad I had gone to the store and traded my new ones for hers.

"Look again," I said anxiously. Instead of wanting to open gifts, I was now totally hooked on the idea of giving.

She smiled shyly, not knowing what to expect next. With one glance into the bag, she was crying. "A telescope! I can't accept this."

"Yes, you can. I only wanted one because you wanted one. You need it; I don't."

She hugged me tightly. I could feel how fast her heart was beating. I closed my eyes and felt a tremendous warmth.

A few months later Carol and her family moved away. Her father had gotten a better job in another town. We swore we'd keep in touch, but it was one of those things you never really do.

When they drove away in their old station wagon, she waved from the back. I really thought I'd never see her again. But God had other plans.

* * *

Ten years later I was working late in the university library when I looked up. There was a lovely, blonde woman with gorgeous but familiar brown eyes. She was staring at me.

"Excuse me," she said softly. "This may sound crazy but—"

"Carol?" I stood, and we clumsily hugged.

"I thought it was you, but I wasn't sure," she said. "It's so good to see you."

We talked about our lives and caught up on everything. She was still interested in astronomy but was going into social work. I was still undecided, but thought I wanted to be a lawyer. We talked as though it was old times.

A few years later we were married.

Sometimes I wonder if I'd never tried to get extra points in school if we still would have met in college. Without her early influence I think I might have become a snob andwouldn't have looked twice at someone who actually had to work to put themselves through school. But how could I have ignored that smile?

Our Christmas Eves are much like her family celebrations. Everyone comes to our house, and we sing. On Christmas morning, after exchanging our few gifts, we go downtown to the shelter where we serve dinner. Instead of teaching our children about Santa and giving them a few years of magic, we teach them about Jesus, giving them a lifetime of miracles.

Above my desk hangs the best Christmas gift I ever got. It's tattered, and you can barely read my name, but it's still perfect. It's my favorite Christmas stocking.

That Christmas of 1973 I believe God looked down on me, lost among all my toys, and saw to it that I got what I really needed.

Julie Rae Rickard, freelance writer, writes from Clearfield, Pennsylvania.

The Ragged Red Coat

Karen A. Williams

She couldn't get those words out of her mind: "Isn't it strange that on Christ's birthday we buy gifts for ourselves instead of for Him?"

Neither could she get Yolanda, that lovely little "seasonal," out of her mind.

I saw her again. Her ragged red coat caught my eye as I drove past the bus stop. The icy December wind seemed to tug at her skinny legs. That coat would never do for a Minnesota winter! Immediately I slowed the station wagon and glanced up into the rearview mirror. Her thin figure was a dark silhouette framed in front of a Christmas display. Yellow letters declaring JOY blinked off and on in the store window.

The little girl waited, last in line. I noticed her sloppy sneakers covered with snow; her gray socks sagging around her ankles. Self-consciously, I curled my toes, snug and warm, in my new fur-lined boots. *Such a lonely looking little girl,* I thought. Only a week left before Christmas, and I suddenly was more aware of poverty. *Why?* I won-

dered. I seemed to notice this at Christmas and practically ignore it at other times.

When I turned the corner, she disappeared from sight. I drove on, anxious to visit Ronghild, my mother-in-law, who had lived in a nursing home since her stroke three months before. It was crazy, but when I saw that Mexican girl I had thought of Ronghild. How my mother-in-law and the little girl connected in my mind, I didn't know. But they did. Clear and sharp. Just the day before, after I had closed my bookstore, I had seen the girl at the drugstore down the street. I remembered how we had smiled at each other. Her beautiful brown eyes were big and full of wonderment, like the eyes of a fawn. Yet I noticed a sadness there, too. As soon as I discovered that, my thoughts had jumped to Ronghild.

At the nursing home I hurried through the reception room. When I entered Ronghild's room she was sitting up in bed. Her thin silver hair framed her round face, and she wore her silk bed jacket. My spirits lifted. "Mom, you look better today!" Smiling, I strode to her bedside. Because of her stroke one hand lay curled and useless on top of the blankets, folded by her side and out of the way of the nurses. Her tiny wedding band flickered a gentle beam of gold on her useless hand.

"Kathy!" she called happily. "You look pretty. You've a new curly permanent." Her words slurred slightly as a result of her stroke. "Are you ready for Christmas?" she asked. Her soft voice held a hint of excitement.

I drew a chair up close to her bed. I remembered how she used to make each holiday so special for everyone. Christmas was always her favorite, and she'd plan weeks ahead what she'd give to each person. When I first married her son, Cal, he used to tease her about giving something to everyone in town.

"Cal's the only one left to buy for. I want to buy him a ski sweater, but he wants a fishing reel." I hated buying gifts that couldn't be used until months later.

Mom leaned closer to me and I smelled the sweet scent of body lotion used for back rubs. "Isn't it strange," she whispered, and I had to crouch forward to hear her, "that on Christ's birthday we buy gifts for ourselves instead of for Him?"

I stiffened. Her unusual question stunned me a little.

Reaching over, she tugged at the sleeve of my gray tweed coat. She was strong and surprisingly persistent with that one good hand. "At church we used to collect food and clothes for the migrant workers. And not just at Christmas time, either." When she said that, a pink flush spread across her dull cheeks.

"I always wondered why migrant workers came to Minnesota," I said.

"Many migrants come here. Picking strawberries and vegetables is a tough job. And those people are cheap labor." Her voice quivered, then rose to a pitch of frustration. "I think it's terrible how we ignore those people who harvest our food!"

I felt slightly bewildered by her wandering conversation.

She sighed and dropped her head back onto the pillow. She spoke wistfully and slowly. "I remember . . . in the summer . . . when I cleaned strawberries I'd find a gray hair tangled in the stems. That strand of silver hair always made me wonder who picked those berries for me."

I felt the need to say something to her, perhaps share my concern, too. "Lately, I've seen a little Mexican girl. Her ragged red coat doesn't look very warm."

"She must be seasonal," Mom nodded.

"What's that?"

"Sometimes a family works at the same farm for the whole harvest. They're called seasonals. And some even try to stay here over the winter. It seldom works out. There aren't many jobs in Spring Grove."

"Time for dinner, Mrs. Swenson." A pleasant nurse set a tray down. and the mouth-watering aroma of roast beef and gravy filled the room.

"I'd better dash for home and get our dinner, too," I said, standing up. My voice shook. It always did that when I had to leave her. A sadness would creep into Mom's eyes when I left. *As if she thinks I won't return,* I thought with gloom.

"Do you know her name?" Ronghild asked.

I looked back, puzzled.

"The little Mexican girl."

"Oh. No, I don't. I've only seen her twice."

"That's too bad," she replied, her voice distant.

I walked outside, shivering in the damp snowfall, and pulled my coat collar up to keep the wet snowflakes from my neck. As the windshield wipers slapped noisily back and forth I felt a strange apprehension, as if I were a person expecting a special gift.

At home the boys met me in the kitchen. "What's for supper?" 12-year-old Daniel asked, his face still ruddy from the cold walk home after delivering newspapers.

"How can you two be so hungry all the time?" I teased.

Eight-year-old Joey poured himself a glass of orange

juice while Daniel grabbed a handful of carrot sticks.

"It's Friday, so we eat early, and we're having tacos. Don't fill up on snacks," I reminded them.

Joey drank his juice, then scooted off downstairs. But Daniel faced me. By his serious expression I knew he had a question. "Tacos—that's Mexican food, isn't it, Mom?"

"Sure, why?" I peeled off the cellophane from the head of lettuce.

"We got a new girl in class. She's Mexican. But Mrs. Sanders said we could use the terms Hispanic or Chicano, too," he said proudly.

I felt a twinge, as if Daniel had touched a spark of electricity within me. "Does she have a red coat?" I felt foolish asking. It couldn't possibly be the same girl, I told myself. Yet I couldn't help inquiring. I set the lettuce aside to drain.

Daniel looked at me blankly and shrugged his shoulders. "I don't know, Mom." He snatched two more carrot sticks and headed after Joey.

For a second I felt a sense of bewilderment. *That little girl keeps popping up in my world today,* I thought.

Cal came home from the lumberyard and laughed as he walked in the door. "I can always tell it's Friday. Paper plates and an early dinner."

I laughed with him. Cal had such an easy humor about him. He never failed to lift my spirits. "If business at my bookstore picks up I'll treat us all to a Friday night out soon," I promised.

After dinner Joey and Daniel hovered near Cal's chair.

"Are we going to the tree farm Sunday to cut down our Christmas tree?" Joey asked. A dab of tomato sauce still clung to his chin.

"You bet," Cal answered, winking at me.

Cutting down our pine tree was a holiday tradition for us. We'd tramp for more than an hour through the fields, drinking in the raw scent of pine and measuring different trees until our legs ached. The right tree always needed *everyone's* approval.

Cal sipped his coffee. He held his mug like a glass because his fingers were too thick to use the handle. I grinned back and studied his hands. Hands are showcases for a person's talents, and I always thought I'd fallen in love with Cal's capable hands first, his personality second.

Soon the boys scampered off to their rooms and Cal stacked the coffee mugs in the dishwasher. "Only a week left for shopping," Cal reminded me. "And you still haven't given me an idea about what to buy for you."

For a minute I let my hands dangle at the edge of the sink. For some reason I couldn't think of one thing I really needed or wanted. "Your mother made a comment today," I told him. "She said that it's strange that on Christ's birthday we buy ourselves gifts instead of giving to Him. I almost cried when she said that. It really hit close to the core of Christmas." I shook my head.

Cal sat down at the kitchen table. "I know what you mean." He fiddled absentmindedly with the candles in the advent wreath. "We're trapped into the same commercialism each year. There's no escaping that."

* * *

Sunday was beautiful. Such a day made life worth living in Minnesota. At 4:00 we drove out to the tree farm. Brilliant afternoon sunshine glistened off the whiteness of the fresh snow. Pure light blinded me, but I loved it. I stared dreamily at the azure sky, a blue canvas dotted with fluffy, puffball clouds. Along the road oak, maple, and pine trees wore feathered snow coats. Such beauty was a fantasy Christmas card, and I wondered how anything could spoil my contentment.

We followed several other cars down the dirt road to Mr. Lindberg's farm. The old farmer wore his familiar fur cap and a red- and black-checkered jacket. He directed traffic down different lanes leading into his pine groves. "Time sure flies, don't it?" he smiled as we piled out of the car. His face wrinkled into tiny crisscrossed lines, like a dried apple doll's face.

"I want a Scotch pine this year." I smiled warmly and gathered twine from the trunk. Cal picked up his hand saw, then handed the boys the green plastic sled they used to haul the cut tree.

"Scotch pine . . . That's the west grove, close by." Mr. Lindberg pointed. "See that little Mexican girl over there by that shack? The Scotch pines run along the migrant barracks. The asparagus fields go beyond that."

I almost gasped out loud. There she was again in that ragged red coat. That child was like a winter phantom, appearing to me every few days.

The boys waved excitedly and trudged off. Cal waited next to me. I squinted and looked past the girl at the gray shack that leaned precariously. Its walls sagged to the left, and the roof drooped as if a giant had used it for a foot stool. I saw a puff of smoke curling up from the chimney pipe.

"Somebody's living in that shack," I remarked incredulously.

"Ya." Mr. Lindberg nodded matter-of-factly. A hard look tightened his face. "Juan Sanchez and his 12-year-old daughter, Yolanda. They're living there this winter." He shrugged. "They're seasonals. Come up here from south Texas to work for me every harvest. I offered Juan a winter job repairing the barracks. He's a good carpenter. Yolanda, his oldest daughter, stayed behind with him." Mr. Lindberg took off his cap and scratched his bald head. "I've the worst luck. Juan fell off a ladder a few weeks back and broke his leg. The girl's been a big help to him."

"*Your* bad luck!" I snapped, dismayed at the farmer's comment. Cal nudged my arm and frowned at me. Mr. Lindberg's surprised look made me flush with embarrassment. But I was shocked by his attitude.

He cleared his throat. "The wife and I can't support another family, Mrs. Swenson." His voice was rough, as if he dared me to challenge him. "I paid Juan a month's wage, even though he can't work. And I let them live in that shack free. Yolanda can find pinecones and scrap wood for fuel." He jammed his cap back on his head, then he walked away.

I stared after him, wondering why I suddenly felt like the guilty one. It really wasn't my problem, I assured myself. But anger rose in my chest. My breath came in short pants, and puffs of icy air floated in front of my face. I tried to calm myself. Mr. Lindberg was right. I had to admit that. He couldn't support two families. Neither could we. *But still,* I thought, *someone should do more to help that migrant man and his daughter.*

"Come on, Kathy," Cal prodded me. "The boys are waiting up ahead."

We plowed through the sparkling snowdrifts.

Around the bend I heard Daniel call out, "Hey, Mom, look who I met."

He and Joey stood on either side of the girl. She blinked her round brown eyes, obviously amazed at the sudden attention.

"Mom, this is Yolanda, the new girl in school I told you about."

"Well, hello," I called. "We've seen each other before. In the drugstore, remember?" A lump rose in my throat as I looked at the child. *The temperature has to be 18 degrees*, I thought wildly. *And she isn't wearing mittens or a hat.* Only that tattered red coat clung to her thin body. Two black braids framed a lovely brown face. Her lips looked raw, chapped from the cold.

"I'm collecting pinecones for the stove," Yolanda said shyly. She picked a fluted cone out of her bag to show us. I noticed her refined hands. I realized I had expected a laborer's hands—rough and calloused. Instead I saw thin, graceful fingers. The hands of an intelligent artist, I immediately judged. Her delicate hands made her poverty even more unfair. Feelings of desperation overwhelmed me. I knew she wouldn't have much of a chance for an education. I raged inside.

Cal seemed to sense my feelings. He put a comforting arm around my shoulders. "How's your father?" he asked.

"He's better. Not so much pain now," Yolanda answered. Anxiously, she glanced back at the shack. "I'd better go. I have to fix Papa supper."

She waved goodbye and picked her way back down the path through the footprints in the snow. She glanced back at me once, and my heart took a painful flip-flop. She had that same sad look that my mother-in-law gave me whenever I left her room. It seemed to ask me if I'd ever come back. It was the connection between them. The reason they always clicked together in my mind.

I watched the girl. She moved like a fawn . . . graceful and so, so fragile.

"Mom!" Joey tugged at my ski-jacket. "How come she doesn't wear a hat or mittens?"

I struggled to force back a sob and couldn't answer.

Cal answered for me. "Some people don't have the money to buy those things."

"But it's cold outside. She'll get frostbite, Mom!" Joey's voice was cross, as if he blamed Cal and me for what Yolanda lacked.

"I wonder what kind of Christmas Yolanda will have?" Daniel asked.

Cal motioned us to walk on ahead. Suddenly a thought pricked my mind. It rapped at me like a woodpecker hammering at a tree. I stopped.

"We buy gifts for each other, but not for Him!" I said the words loudly.

They all paused and stared back at me.

"Grandma said that," I announced to the boys. "Cal, wait a minute," I called, even though he hadn't moved. "We haven't bought each other a gift yet, right?"

"I know, but what does that have to do with anything?"

My words tumbled out so fast I could hardly keep up with the idea exploding inside of me. Now I could explain that apprehension I felt about waiting for a gift. Now I knew what that gift was. It was the gift of giving. "Instead of buying each other gifts, Cal, let's take that money and buy Yolanda a new coat!"

"You mean, not even buy each other a Christmas gift this year?"

"We'll buy a gift for someone who really needs one," I explained. "By giving a gift like that we'll be giving to Christ. That's what your mother meant. I'm sure of it. And it's a way to escape that Christmas commercialism we complain about."

For an instant Cal's face looked so firm that I felt disappointment sink in my heart. His practicality often nudged my frivolous notions aside. Then his serious expression melted like candle wax, and he grinned from ear to ear. "That's a great idea, Kathy."

"Can I give her a new hat and mittens?" Joey asked. "I've saved $5."

"They'll cost more than that," Daniel said, "but I want to help, too. I'll put in $5 from my paper route." His face beamed.

"On Christmas Eve let's leave the packages secretly outside their shack. A person's pride is a delicate thing," I whispered. I felt so wonderful, so filled with Christmas that tears welled up in my eyes. As I blinked, ringlets of light sparkled like colored Christmas bulbs and danced across the pine grove.

"Kathy, how come you're such a smart lady?" Cal teased. He opened his arms and I instinctively drew within his embrace.

"I had a good teacher. Your mom always put Christ first. Now I know why."

Karen A. Williams wrote for family and inspirational magazines during the second half of the twentieth century.

Evensong

Joseph Leininger Wheeler

A lonely woman, a troubled author, a father-hungry little girl, a lost journal, God . . . and "Evensong."

PRELUDE

Constance gazed at her 7-year-old daughter through pain-racked eyes. The miniature edition of herself stood there, staring out the window, lost in thought. Her resemblance to Constance was striking, even to the pain etched on the child's face.

"Mommy, do you think Father really loves me?"

"How could he help it, dear?"

"Mommy! You're not answering my question!" Serious eyes peered out, framed by long golden hair.

"Well, I *think* he does—in his own way."

[Sigh] "'In his own way' somehow doesn't make me feel very loved."

"Doesn't *my* love count?"

[Leaping up from the armchair and giving her a strangling hug] "Of course! You know it does! It's—it's just that I want my, uh, father to love me, too. Well, not father—what I *really* want is a daddy. Someone who will laugh with me, joke with me; I can muss his hair, sit on his lap, listen to him read stories to me. And somebody who won't go away but will stay with us always. Oh, Mommy, I didn't mean to make you sad. Don't cry!"

"It's all right, precious, it's just that I, too, wish things were, uh, different."

"When do I see Father?"

"In two weeks. He's gone to Switzerland."

"But he *knew* I'd be here today. He sent our tickets. He got us this room in this hotel that I love [clambering onto the chair by the window], where I can see that beautiful bridge."

"I know, dear. Yes, he knew. I suppose something came up."

"With Father something's *always* coming up."

"Well, dear, at least you and I can have fun together."

"But what are we going to *do?*"

And that was the quandary. She'd been afraid this would happen—again. Ah, what forces she had set in motion 12 years before, back when she thought beauty meant happiness. Every beauty pageant she had ever entered, she won, even the one at Northern Arizona University in snowy Flagstaff.

And how excited she'd been when he had noticed her. The buzz of campus—a real, live Earl, and said to be filthy rich. Good-looking, too. Came out here to see the "Old West." Even wore cowboy boots and a Stetson.

And then, when it got serious, she'd been too star struck to delve beneath the surface. Just think, as a countess she'd be addressed as "Right Honorable" and "My Lady." Her eldest son would be called a viscount while his father lived, her other sons would be lords, and her daughters, ladies. Oh, it was just too exciting!

But when Robert flew her to England to meet his widowed mother, she experienced her first reservations. Lavish apartments in London, a visit to the Castle in Scotland, parties, balls, and formal dinners. Robert's mother was rather cold to her, and Constance once overheard her saying to her son, "A pretty little thing, but not much in the way of family connections. If she had money that would be some comfort, at least, but she doesn't even have *that!*"

Constance fled to her room in tears. Robert followed, assuring her that nothing else mattered but the two of them. Surely, if they loved each other "Mum" would come around.

So they married, and she became a countess. She became almost giddy with the whirlwind of parties and socializing. Robert seemed proud of her, and her beauty, coupled with her title, opened all doors to her.

Then a child was born to them—a girl, much to Robert's disgust. In fact, he didn't seem to even want the baby around him. When Constance refused to turn her baby girl over to a nanny, that was the last straw. Robert stormed out of their bedchamber and, for all practical purposes, out of her life. "Mum" did not come around either. More and more, Robert stayed at the club or in his London bachelor's apartments. She rarely knew where he was. It might be Monte Carlo (his crowd loved to gamble), he might be away on business, he might be at a polo match, horse racing, or chasing foxes. He might be anywhere in the world but home with her. *Home?* What a laugh! She had no home. Neither did little Beth. All that was bad enough, but then came the tabloid photos of Robert with one woman after another—but never with her.

Finally, when she could handle no more of his public mockery of their marriage, she applied for divorce. Instead of its bringing him to his senses, he encouraged it. Once final, he gave her a generous settlement and suggested she move back to America with "Elizabeth" (he never called her "Beth"). Within six months he was married again, this time to an old-time family friend, one who reveled in high society, and, not coincidentally, was the daughter of a lord. Within five years two sons came to them. As for his daughter, he condescended to see her only once a year. And his new wife made it clear that the little girl was to come and go quickly. Her sons would inherit most of the estate and assets. Getting the message, her stepbrothers were cool to Beth as well.

Only after the fact did Constance realize another thing she'd lost: her relationship with God. There had been no place for God in the whirlwind of pleasure eddying around her and Robert. And without God to anchor in, the marriage so full of promise at the start, instead self-destructed.

So, deeply wounded, she took Beth and moved back to America, to old Santa Fe, where she finished college and did internships in rare books, art, and antiques prior to establishing her own business. And she and Beth sought out God. Still lovely, Constance was besieged by suitors, but she didn't dare get close to any of them. She no longer trusted her judgment where men were concerned. Besides, there was little Beth—she must not put her at risk again.

Suddenly she became aware that night had fallen, the lights on Tower Bridge had come on, Beth had fallen asleep, and she was alone with her thoughts. *Alone*. More and more in recent months she had felt that aloneness— a sense that half of her was missing. At night the bed was big, and there was no one to cuddle up to, to put his arms around her, to talk with her, to laugh with her, to love her. And Beth needed more than just a father. As she'd just made abundantly clear, she needed—*desperately needed*—a daddy. She was such an adorable, precocious 7-year-old. She read on the sixth-grade level (and read omnivorously). Worldly-wise beyond her years, this child was yet innocent, idealistic, and intensely loving.

O God, Constance prayed, *You see what a mess I've made of my life. But You also know how sorry I am! I know I don't deserve it, but I'm so lonely, Lord. Is there somewhere my soul's other half? Is there someone out there who'd be my soul mate, and who loves You as much as I do? Who would unconditionally love Beth, too? I know You've got far more important things to do than bail out a foolish woman, but O Lord, please find him for me.*

For some time she just sat there in silence, her brain in neutral. Softly she rose and walked toward the window. Inadvertently she bumped the dresser, and something fell behind it. *Oh no, not my passport!* But it was. Very carefully, so as not to wake Beth, she slowly pulled the dresser away from the wall, reached behind, and found—not just her passport, but something else: a leather case.

That woke Beth. "Mommy, what are you doing?" she asked sleepily.

Constance turned on several lamps and sat down on the bed. "Come over here, dear, and let's find out what's in this thing."

It was indeed a case, slim and of high-grade leather.

Some other occupant of Room 507 must have bumped this same dresser with the same results. Only that person left without noticing that the case was missing. Then later, upon discovering its loss, would not have known where he'd left it. At least she assumed the owner was a he—the case looked masculine.

"Open it up, Mommy!" demanded Beth.

She did. "Well, what do you know!" she exclaimed. "A journal!"

"What's *that?*" asked Beth.

"Oh, it's a diary. . . . Just like yours, and just like mine."

"Oh, goody! Let's read it!"

"Do you really think we ought to?" Constance responded doubtfully.

"Of *course!* How else will we find out who it belongs to?" the little girl answered. "Besides, you *know* you're going to snoop—you always do. And you know I'm going to snoop—I always do. So we might as well snoop together!"

Chuckling at their inability to resist snooping, they fluffed up their pillows and settled down to read. "Read it out loud!" ordered Beth. So she did.

"JOURNAL OF WILLIAM HARRISON."

"It's a man. I knew it would be," interrupted Beth.

"DAY ONE: On Board British Air, Denver to London."

"Oh goody! He's from Denver. We've been there."

"Perhaps, dear. He may be from somewhere else."

"I don't really know what it is that I'm fleeing from, or what I'm expecting to find in Old England. I only know that a Higher Power willed it.

"Nights have been long in recent days, weeks, and months.

I've had such a hard time getting to sleep. It has been almost six years since that terrible July night when a truck driver veered across the median and smashed into our Lexus, killing my lovely Julia almost instantly. Oh, he was contrite, that truck driver was, and admitted to the police that he'd skipped several mandatory rest stops—and had fallen asleep at the wheel. But his being sorry couldn't bring my beloved Julia back."

"How sad! The poor man!" said Beth, sighing.

Constance continued reading.

"At first, the pain of losing her was so intense it blotted out time and reality. It was like a nightmarish movie that never got to its screen credits at the end. Because there was no end. Because this was real, not mere fiction. Time after time, I'd reach for her in the night, only to find once more that she was not there, would never be there again. That I was alone in the midst of my life journey. Alone at 33."

"Thirty-three what, Mommy?"

"Thirty-three years old, dear."

"Oh."

"Toward the end of the second year the anguish began to diminish. If it hadn't, it would have killed me. Early that October, as Bob and I were hiking in the Grand Tetons (what would I have done without close friends like him?), it came to me that my mind and body were finally un-numbing, coming back to an awareness of life, of its beauty. The singing and cascading creek, joyfully leapfrogging its way down to the Snake River."

"Is the Snake River in Colorado?"

"No, dear. He was hiking in Wyoming. Maybe we'll find out if he lives there."

"The always curious, hyper, and scolding squirrels, never silent or still if they could help it. The ubiquitous magpies that would follow us all the way, demanding handouts—"

"Stop, Mommy. What's, uh, u-biqui—"

"Ubiquitous, darling, means that they're everywhere. You remember those big black and white birds, don't you?"

"Oh, yes—they're such pests! One even ate out of my hand. Felt funny!" she giggled.

"The wind . . . soughing in the pines . . . brought me my first peace."

"What's soughing?"

"You know, dear; don't you remember how you love to hear the pines whispering in the wind?"

"Oh, yes! Sometimes it sounds like a waterfall—a long way off!"

"Well put, my dear. You may grow up to be a writer someday."

"Mommy, I like the way he writes. Wonder if he writes books?"

"Could be, dear."

"I turned to my hiking companion and said, 'Bob, I've just had an epiphany.'

"Stolid, unimaginative Bob muttered, 'Had a what?'

"'An epiphany.'"

"'What's that?'"

Beth chortled, "Oh, that's funny! He's old, and he doesn't know what big words mean either!"

Her mother smiled and continued reading.

"'Oh, sorry. It's, uh, a sudden realization of a great truth, an unexpected insight into life.'"

"'Oh?'"

"'Yes. I just realized that my life is not over. That it will go on . . . and that there's still beauty all around me. And joy. And that I've wasted far too much time already. It's time to begin writing again, too.'"

"I *knew* it!"

"I suspected it, too, dear."

"'*'Bout time*,' agreed Bob, always stingy with words."

Beth's laugh sounded like tinkling chimes in a soft wind.

"It was indeed ''bout time,' but Scripture reminds us that there's a time for everything.

But in life, the price of skipping a stage is a delayed time bomb later on, so I had to work through grief in order to be able to reenter life, to become productive again.

"It would have helped had we been blessed with children. Julia had longed for a boy, I for a girl. But it was not to be. Just a week before that wreck, for the first time we had discussed the possibility of adoption. Oh, the seraphic look on her dear face when I agreed to initiate the long process of adopting a child. We hadn't yet decided whether the first would be a boy or a girl—but we did want both eventually.

"But we had no child as yet, so I endured my grief alone—and longer than was good for me. But now, at long last, I came out into the blinding light at the end of the serpentine tunnel. Out to life."

"Mommy, stop! I want to think before you go on. He says so much in a few words that my mind gets too full."

"I know what you mean, dear."

"Let me think, and don't rush me. . . . Oh, now I know what I want to say: he loved her, didn't he?"

"Yes, dear."

"And he would have loved a little girl (if he'd adopted her) . . . almost as much."

"Just as much, darling."

"More than Father loves me?"

"Oh, honey!" Constance took Beth into her arms—she just couldn't bear to admit the cruel answer out loud. Instead, she returned to the journal. "Let's see, where was I? Oh yes, there's extra space here—it means time has passed, and it's now later than it was."

"In time much healing has come. And happiness. I've found both in hard work, in getting my mind off of self and focusing on others instead. God has been good—has respected my space. Has picked up His end of the phone when I've called. For a long time I called Him only once in a while; then it was oftener and oftener. Now we never hang up at all."

"What does he mean, Mommy?"

"He means, dear, that God is always in his heart, his thoughts, so he talks to Him all the time now."

"Like we do with each other?"

"Yes, like that."

"Oh."

"Lately I've been asking God if it's His will that I remain alone the rest of my life. I'm still young, could still be a husband again—a dad. But it scares me to think about going through the relationship meat grinder again."

"Huh? Is he trying to be funny?"

Constance laughed as she hadn't in months. Finally, wiping her eyes, she chuckled, "He means, dear, that courtship is tough work, and it's easy to get sort of chopped up by the other person."

"Like Father chopped *you* up?" Then, taking a look at her mother's blanched, pain-ridden face, she rose on her knees and hugged her, murmuring, "I didn't mean to hurt you, Mommy! Forgive me?"

"Of course, dear . . . but it hurts because you're right. There have indeed been times when I too felt more than a little chopped up. Now, let me read on."

"*I look around me, and almost no relationship seems to last very long anymore. In fact, most people my age don't value the institution of marriage.*"

* * *

Constance, realizing that this section was too deep for her child and that Beth was already drifting off to sleep again, tenderly tucked the spread under her chin, kissed her on the forehead, and returned to the journal, determined to get beyond this section before she read any more aloud.

"*It's all downhill from there, nothing more to look forward to. It's only, I wonder how long we'll be able to stand each other?*"

* * *

"*And the ones who do marry don't take it very seriously. First bump, and they're 'outa here.' Oh, of course there are many who miraculously make it through somehow. But, if they do, it's no thanks to cinema, TV, or the print media. Where are our children to find traditional role models? Where are they going to see portrayed decent men and women who really believe promises such as 'Until death do us part'? Rarely do such people appear on either the big or the small screen anymore. When they do, they are mocked, they are ridiculed. That really scares me. How does one dare to bring up a child in such a dissolute age?*"

* * *

This was the end of that day's entry. Constance closed the journal, put on her nightgown, slipped into the bed closest to the window, and looked out at the Tower Bridge, ablaze with lights, her thoughts tumbling like clothes in a dryer.

Two hours later, she was still wide awake. Jet lag—and this unknown voice in the journal—precluded sleep. Finally she gave up, turned on her small bedside reading light, and reached for the journal.

DAY TWO: Still on Board British Air to London

"*Left Jackson Hole early yesterday morning, drove all day, and boarded this great plane early last evening in Denver. And is it ever full! Furthermore, there are more babies and kids per capita than I've ever seen on a plane. What a night it has been! Rarely did silence last more than minutes. Almost continually, babies whimpered, sobbed, cried, or screamed.*

"*Just across the aisle from me are two young British families. Two brothers. They've been skiing in Colorado. One of them has a toddler (1¹/₂-2 years old) who has been out of control for hours at a time. Screams so loudly he periodically turns scarlet and gags. The parents strap him into a car seat attached to a pull-down platform, and then just sit there, blithely ignoring the continual screaming. They don't touch him, take him into their arms, speak to him, or address whatever the problem is.*

"*Finally, absolutely exhausted, landed at Gatwick International Airport. Took a while to get through customs and pick up my luggage. Then boarded the shuttle to London.*

"*THISTLE TOWER HOTEL*

"*Wasn't able to write in the shuttle, but now I'm all checked in at this beautiful hotel on the river Thames. Outside my window is the majestic Tower Bridge. A few hundred feet from the hotel is a piece of history I've heard about and read* about all my life—the ancient Tower of London. It all seems like a dream. I keep thinking, This can't be real!

"I still don't know why God sent me on this trip, but I'm convinced it was for a reason. My part, as I see it, is to follow my itinerary and chronicle my reactions. I've read that unless one immediately writes down one's travel-related observations, they are lost.

"So before they become hazy, I'll write down my first impressions of this, America's mother country. First, I can't get over driving on the wrong side of the road. Gives me the heebie-jeebies! All these thousands of vehicles constricting these narrow lanes crowd each other in a continual game of chicken. Yet no one seems angry or succumbs to road rage like we see in America. Time and again, I saw drivers brake to a quick stop and wave another driver into the traffic flow. And motorcyclists jauntily speed along between the opposing streams of traffic!

"It is cold and drizzly, and the land looks green and damp—everything looks mossy. Instead of fences, hedgerows on property lines. Lots of birds. Here and there, Beatrix Potter-type houses, and large country estates. Lots of busses, small trucks, and cars; very few SUVs, probably because petrol costs about $5 a gallon! Stoplights the reverse of ours: red, yellow, then green. Houses and businesses are smaller than I'm used to, with precious little space separating them. Taxis everywhere, but small and charcoal-colored rather than yellow. Signs point to places sounding strangely familiar: Heathrow Airport, Wimbledon, Arundel.

"As congestion increased I sensed we were moving into London proper, the heart of the British Commonwealth. Again, I was impressed with the quietness—no blaring of horns, and rarely did I hear sirens. Then came the Houses of Parliament and that most familiar of sights, Big Ben. Oh, and that upstart: the Eye, a Ferris wheel towering more than 400 feet into the skyline, on the banks of the Thames. They say it takes 40 minutes to make one rotation. A wildly popular tourist attraction with the best view in London.

"Sense impressions came at me from all directions, and faster than I could assimilate them. The old and the new, the past and the present, coexist side by side. The streets are narrow and crooked, which is only to be expected as most were constructed hundreds and hundreds of years ago.

"And at last the Thistle Hotel, 650 rooms overlooking the Thames and St. Catherine's Marina. Checked in, then up to room 507. Outside, dead center out my window, is the Tower Bridge, new by London terms (built late in the 1800s). Upriver just a little is moored a great British warship, vintage World War II. And outside is the unceasing flow of the London anthill.

"Sleep deprivation catches up with me at last, so I crawl in.

Sleep deprivation getting to Constance too, she scanned the next few pages, put down the journal, turned off the light, and drifted off into dreams.

* * *

Constance was awakened by soft arms around her neck, kisses, and importuning: "Wake up, Mommy, wake up!"

Stretching languorously, her mother sleepily retorted, "What on earth for?

"The journal! I want to see what comes next. You didn't . . . you didn't? You did read on after I went to sleep! Shame, shame, shame on you!"

"Yes, dear, but just a little—the philosophical part. I

stopped when I came to the part I knew you'd like. Apparently Mr. Harrison went to see an interesting place in London each day he was here. What do you say that each morning we read about his experiences there, and then go follow him and see if we agree with what he wrote. Wouldn't that be fun?"

"Yes! Let's."

"All right. As soon as we get back from breakfast, we'll begin."

DAY THREE: The Tube and the Double-Decker

"I know! Let's pretend we're tourists too—never been in London before."

"And see if we can learn something new?" added her mother.

"Right!"

"Slept late as rain still falling. Breakfast at hotel's second-floor Tower Restaurant. Around the circular walls are pictures of famous and infamous historical residents of the Tower of London."

"What are infamous people?" asked Beth, wrinkling her forehead.

"They are famous people who were bad.

"Oh."

"But most are admired people who didn't deserve to die by the axe. People such as the ill-fated wives of Henry VIII, Sir Walter Raleigh, etc. I look forward to seeing the Tower later on during my visit.

"But I dedicated today to learning how to get around this vast city. Walked several hours before I finally found out how to get a week's ticket on the Tube. Then descended deep into the bowels of the earth—"

"He's funny," giggled Beth.

"—and boarded the subway, the system of travel that keeps London alive. Stops are close together, so there's no need to take surface transportation. Inside the cars people are polite to each other. They read, they speak in low tones; some sit, some stand. Quite a polyglot mixture of nationalities."

"Polyglot?"

"It means *many* nationalities, dear."

"Lots of women in London's workforce, and lots of tourists, even in off-season. Brits call this process 'tubing.'

"After surfacing, couldn't help noticing the sheer size of the crowds flooding the city like so many rushing ants. And they're all in such a hurry to get somewhere! Even though I walk at a rather fast pace (faster than the average in the U.S.), they pass me half again as fast. Brits hurry everywhere! Not surprisingly, according to a London newspaper I read this morning, 80 percent of Brits suffer from extreme stress. Many physical breakdowns because of it.

"Of what value is a life, I wonder, that is torqued up to such a frantic pace that there's no time to think or dream; no time to nurture, to make deep friendships, to grow in love, to draw ever closer to God?

"No time."

"What's nurture? I kind of think I know what it means, but I'm not sure."

"Well, it means to nourish or take care of something or someone. It also means to help raise a child, like I'm trying to do with you, dear."

"Boarded 'Big Bus' after I learned how to use the Tube. Being it was bitterly cold, stayed on the lower level. Got a kick out of the guides. Each thinks he's (or she's) a stand-up comedian. The first one really knew his stuff. There wasn't a thing

THE TOWER BRIDGE

death with their horses, dogs, and guns.

"It's an interesting system: their most powerful leader is not even chosen by the people but by party leaders. So when the people get fed up enough, they throw everyone out of office at once!

"And I'm intrigued by their terms: 'bonnet' for car hood, 'bloke' for man, 'to let' for 'to rent,' 'lift' for elevator, and (my favorite) 'spend-a-penny' for the street-side john."

Beth covered her mouth in her failure to keep from laughing.

"And now it's night again, and I sit by my window staring out at that dreamlike bridge. It's getting to me. It's magical."

* * *

"Well, honey, did he get it right?"

"Oooh! I'm tired. But he was right. People are polite to each other, politer than at home. And they do hurry. Remember when I tried to keep up with one woman? I had to *run!*"

"Yes, I agree. And he was right about the bus guides, too. It was so funny to see our guide swing out of the bus like Tarzan on a vine, on the way to 'spend-a-penny.'"

DAY FOUR: Kensington Palace

It was a new day in London, and the skies were cloudy. After breakfast, Constance opened the journal and began reading.

"Breakfast in the Tower Restaurant. Really full today as several bus loads of tourists came in last night. Food good, as always.

we went by that he couldn't identify. Had a wicked sense of humor—and his favorite targets were the Royal Family and the Prime Minister. Right now the Prime Minister is really getting it for his reversal on family values and his waffling on fox hunting. He came into office trumpeting the need for strong marriages and families, but so many of his associates now have failed marriages that they've all caved in on the issue. And the gentry are really furious at him for telling them they shouldn't run poor foxes to

110

"Took the Tube to Kensington Palace. In summer they say Kensington Gardens are one of the beauty spots of the city, but you wouldn't know it this time of year. Wind cut like a knife.

"William and Mary lived in this palace. But as I walked through the vast rooms it was hard for me to conceive of anyone actually living here (so large, so formal, so ornate, and then so full of staff, courtiers, and visitors). When could rulers who lived here have been themselves? When (and where) could they have spent time with their mates, their children?"

"I feel the same way about Father's castle. Even where he lives in London. It's not comfy, but, uh, sort of like being in a museum," Beth mused, almost as if talking to herself.

"Saw the Princess Di clothing collection. Beautiful dresses! After her breakup with Prince Charles, Di and her two sons lived on the other side of Kensington Palace. I felt sorry for her for it was quipped that Charles was the only man in the world not in love with her. The idol of the world, but not of her own husband!

"Can never forget getting up in the wee hours of the morning to see the wedding spectacular on television. The whole world watched that fairytale unfold. But even then, Charles had to be prompted to show her any affection.

"I wonder if he's really capable of love. Never will I forget the story of the little Charles who ran toward his mother, after she and his father had been on a six-month round-the-world cruise on the royal ship, "Britannia." Half a year to a child is forever! So he ran into her arms. Well, not quite. She stopped his rush by sticking out her right hand for a handshake! How could a child who was treated so coldly by his own mother be capable of real love with wife and children?"

"That's the way Father is with me," mused Beth. "Sort of cold. It hurts. He doesn't even smile at me most of the time. Makes me afraid of him. Doesn't act like he loves me at all."

Constance remained mute.

"And many Brits send their boys off to all-male boarding schools in order to 'toughen them up.' Thus they grow up without the softening influence of their mothers.

"Several months ago I saw a group of British tourists in Jackson Hole. I was curious enough to strike up a conversation with them. Apparently they had all left their wives and children back in England, preferring to share their holidays with old schoolmates instead.

"Something's not quite right here."

Constance stopped reading and put the journal down, a pensive look on her face. "He's right, Beth. When a man's wife and children take second place to the schoolmates of his youth, something is most definitely wrong!

"I find myself fascinated by British newspapers. They reflect a world view that is decidedly continental. America's not mentioned much, and rarely in a complimentary fashion. Not that I blame them—we export so much of the seamy side of life."

* * *

"It's 1:00 in the morning, and I can't sleep. So I look out the window at that glorious Tower Bridge, all lit up like a Christmas tree. I see the deep purple, streaked with silver and gold of the river, the people still walking under umbrellas on the banks and on the bridge, the ghostly headlights of cars, trucks, and buses. Where are they all going?

"I'm lonely. Oh, how I wish I had someone to share all

this beauty with. Someone to talk with, commune with, to be my other half, to love."

* * *

Upon their return from Kensington Palace, again there was only silence, each sitting there by the window, each harboring thoughts that were too heavy to ride the flimsy rails of speech.

DAY FIVE: St. Paul's Cathedral.

Uncharacteristically somber after a restless night, mother and daughter wondered what the writer would have to say on this day.

"I've picked up quite a collection of books and pamphlets about places I plan to see. By reading them ahead of time I'll be able to fill in gaps, history-wise, or correct misperceptions ahead of time.

"St. Paul's. All my life I've wanted to see it, experience it. Once, in a history class, a teacher showed us some World War II newsreels. Never will I forget the voice of Edward R. Murrow, the sounds of anti-aircraft guns, the wailing sirens, the bombs exploding—and searchlights spearing the night. And, invariably, somewhere in the newsreel there would be the dome of St. Paul's. And to contemporaries who watched those newsreels, as long as St. Paul's was still there, England was still there—and not yet did Hitler rule the world."

"Who's Hitler, Mommy?"

"A very bad man, dear, who was responsible for the death of millions of innocent people."

"Oh."

"Outside St. Paul's—and the pigeons were still there! It's funny—what did I think of as I looked up at that imposing façade and long flight of steps? A freckle-faced little boy and a pixyish little girl, pigeons, and 'Let's go fly a kite.'"

"Mary Poppins! He's talking about Mary Poppins, Mommy!"

"Mary Poppins comes back to me, a film I've seen over and over.

"Inside St. Paul's; its immensity staggers. The only comparable cathedral dome in the world is St. Peter's in Rome."

Constance read on as Harrison told the long tumultuous history of the cathedral, with antecedents all the way back to 604 A.D. Again and again it had been destroyed or ravaged—by fires, by Vikings, by the soldiers of Oliver Cromwell's Commonwealth, and by the Great Fire of London in 1666. Today's St. Paul's was designed by the great architect, Sir Christopher Wren, immediately after that fire.

"These walls have seen the funerals of Admiral Horatio Nelson, the Duke of Wellington, and Winston Churchill; the marriage of Charles and Diana, the celebration of Queen Victoria's Diamond Jubilee, and Queen Elizabeth II's Silver Jubilee. Handel and Mendelssohn played on this great organ.

"When I finally walked out of the cathedral it was with a feeling that one of the missing pieces of my life had been found."

Later that evening, Beth pensively observed, "I wish—"

"Wish *what*, dear?" tenderly prompted her mother.

"I wish we could have seen Mr. Harrison when he stood there looking at the pigeons . . . but thinking of Mary Poppins."

DAY SIX: The British Museum

Beth grimaced when her mother read the heading. Not another museum! But perhaps he would somehow make it sound interesting. After quite a bit of history, which Beth found beyond her, came these words:

"Couldn't help noticing all the children. Led by their teachers, boys and girls lay on the floor and on benches, lean against tombs, gaze into glass cases, make relief drawings, take copious notes, listen to lectures. To them the great museum was one vast schoolroom—it was history come alive. How I wish I had a child of my own. How wonderful it would be to bring her here and share these treasures with her!"

Unnoticed by her reading mother, a tear trickled down Beth's cheek.

"What was most significant of all to me? Undoubtedly that it reaffirmed one's faith in the Bible. For centuries skeptics discounted the Bible, maintaining that much of it was but myth, that many of the nations appearing in its pages never existed at all. The Hittites, for instance—no record of such a people! Yet here in this museum is archeological proof of the Hittite Empire.

"As for Assyria, dominating its section of the museum are massive human-headed, winged bulls (heavy enough to sink a ship). It suddenly hit me as I stared at them that Jonah must have seen—and perhaps even touched—these (or ones like them) as he walked up and down the broad streets of Nineveh, declaring, "In only 40 days this great city will be destroyed!"

"The Jonah who was swallowed by a whale?" asked Beth, wide-eyed.

"The very same, dear."

"Wow!"

"But the Museum's Holy Grail is the Rosetta Stone."

"What's the 'Holy Grail'?"

"It's a very sacred object associated with our Lord that Knights of the Round Table (according to tradition) longed to find, would give their very lives to find."

"Oh."

"Few in this throng knew enough history to seek it out—even some of the guards didn't seem to know about it. Finally, I found it, calmly blending in with the rest of antiquity in a simple glass case. Hard to believe that this small stone with three kinds of writing on it could be one of the most valuable things on this planet. Up to its discovery in 1799 no one had a clue as to understanding the two languages of ancient Egypt (hieroglyphics and demotic). But here on this stone was one text, in hieroglyphics, demotic, and ancient Greek. With Greek as a key, repeated in this stone, scholars have now unlocked the entire history and culture of ancient times."

Beth asked plaintively, "When we get there you'll show it to me and explain?"

"Yes, dear."

"But the artifact I searched for the longest you had to know by name, and ask again and again where it could be found. Suddenly, there it was—the 2,000-year-old Portland Vase, only 9^1/$_3$ inches tall but one of the world's most precious works of art, the inspiration for Josiah Wedgwood's great line of Greek-inspired china, pottery, and crockery. The single most famous cameo-glass vessel to have survived from ancient times.

"You have a cameo pin, don't you, Mommy?"

"Yes, I do. And we both love it."

"The base is deep cobalt blue, and the cameo glass applied to it depicts mythological love and marriage. The artistic detail is so exquisite it takes your breath away. Perhaps the Apostle

Paul may have seen this vase in his travels.

"The vase has been on display since 1810, and thousands from all over the world have thronged to see it. One of those who drank in its beauty and miraculous preservation was the English poet, John Keats, who, in his famous 'Ode on a Grecian Urn,' concluded with these words:

"'When old age shall this generation waste,
　　Thou shalt remain, in midst of other woe
　Than ours, a friend to man, to whom thou sayest,
　　"Beauty is truth, truth beauty"—that is all
　　　Ye know on earth, and all ye need to know.'

"Only months later the short tragic story of Keats' life was over.

"I have seen so much this day my mind is a blur. Felt like a time traveler swept thousands of years into the past. Each of these artifacts was touched, molded, caressed, admired by men, women, and children in other times—as alive once as I am today. Today telescoped Time in my mind.

"I shall come back to this place."

This time it was the mother who spoke first. "He knows a lot, doesn't he? History, literature, architecture, art. . . ."

"A *lot?* He seems to know everything! How lucky she'll be."

"Who, dear?"

"His little girl—when he gets her."

* * *

"Well, it was quite a day, wasn't it?"

"Yes, Mommy—but my feet hurt!"

"Mine do, too."

"But you know what? I think I learned a lot today—

a lot more than I'd have learned, uh—"

"If we hadn't had the journal?"

"Yes."

DAY SEVEN: The Tower of London

"Where do we go today, Mommy?"

"Right next door: the Tower of London."

"Good, 'cuz my feet are worn out."

"A stunningly beautiful blue-sky day it has been! Perfect for taking in the ancient Tower of London. Even though it isn't tourist season, it was crowded. Hard to imagine that those walls date clear back to William the Conqueror in 1066. It has been everything: royal palace, fortress, prison, place of execution, arsenal, royal mint, menagerie, and repository of the Crown Jewels.

"The Yeoman Warders (beefeaters) who herd visitors through the castle are extremely good at what they do, which is to bring history alive. Had always assumed that the Tower (called the 'White Tower') was complete in itself, not that it was the center portion of the strongest castle in England.

"Like most visitors, what I most wanted to see was the Crown Jewels, but couldn't help thinking as I gazed at all those diamonds, emeralds, rubies, pearls, and gold that even those do not guarantee happiness but rather the reverse. According to an old aphorism, 'Uneasy is the head that wears a crown.'"

"What's that?"

"An aphorism? Oh, it's a quotation, a folk saying."

"Saw room after room, chock full of history, but what moved me most were the people who lived and died within those walls. So many famous people died here, had their heads chopped off in the courtyard. A number of queens: Anne

114

Boleyn, Catherine Howard, Lady Jane Grey. Martyrs such as Sir Thomas More and Bishop John Fisher. Royal favorites such as Robert Devereux and Sir Walter Raleigh. Spent quite a bit of time in the two rooms in the Bloody Tower where Raleigh spent so many years of his life (13 years just during his longest incarceration there).

"As I looked out into the courtyard at the same view Raleigh saw every time he looked out the window, again there came to me a sense of the past elastically tied to the present. All my life I've been reading biography, history, and historical fiction in which the Tower of London plays a key role. 'And he was taken off to the Tower' was a common way of saying he would soon be dead. But only after seeing the actual castle (virtually impregnable) does fact validate fiction in my mind.

"I feel very subdued and melancholy this night as I stare out at the bridge named after the Tower of London. It has not been a particularly happy day, yet in another respect it has been one of the most informative and insightful days of my life."

* * *

"My feet are just as tired as yesterday."

"Is that all?"

"You mean, did I like it? Yes. . . . And did he tell the story true? Yes. He made me think."

"How, dear?"

"Well, that crowns don't make you happy. And all the crowns in the world couldn't make up for being locked up so many years—like poor Raleigh was."

DAY EIGHT: Westminster Abbey

"So, where to today, Mommy?"

"Let's see . . . Westminster Abbey."

"There's so much more I want to see in London, but time precludes that. However, I've saved one day—and all of it is going to be devoted to the single most important historic building in Great Britain—Westminster Abbey.

"It was here that then Princess Elizabeth married Prince Philip (in 1947); it was here that she was crowned Elizabeth II; and it was here that the whole world watched and sobbed as the beautiful Diana, Princess of Wales, finally found peace."

"I remember, Mommy. It was so sad! Remember? We both cried.

"I'll *always* remember, dear."

"Westminster Abbey dates back over a thousand years to 950-960. A hundred years later, King Edward the Confessor decided to make Westminster the focal center of the kingdom. When William, Duke of Normandy, defeated Harold at the Battle of Hastings in 1066, the English monarchy became French. William was crowned in Westminster Abbey.

"As an historian of ideas, I'm fascinated by periods. Future historians looking back at our time will no doubt classify the twentieth century as the Age of Skyscrapers (or computers, of course). But the first millennium spawned the Great Age of Faith during which Europe's soaring Gothic cathedrals were built. They started in France, spread across the channel to England, then to Spain and all across Europe, reaching their peak during the years 1100 to 1400. I'm amazed at how it all seemed to happen at once. What made those great perpendicular Gothic cathedrals possible was a simple wall-supporting device called the "flying buttress." Thanks to it, cathedrals could leap 100 to 150 feet into the sky, and walls could be mostly glass.

"God was preeminent in the lives of Europeans then; the

Crusades certainly proved that. Life expectancy was low, disease wiped out most of those who became ill, chances were that most women would die of childbirth complications, and wars were frequent. In such a world of uncertainty God was the only constant, thus the yearnings of the people were reflected in their Gothic cathedrals, each a community effort. Westminster, Salisbury, Coventry, Rheims, Chartres, Notre Dame, Cologne, Toledo, Barcelona, and so many more, all were born during this brief period of spiritual rebirth. To my way of thinking, mankind has never created a more beautiful type of structure. And look—almost a thousand years later most are still standing! Before I die I'd like to worship in each one.

"Westminster is a queen among them. What must it have been in its glory days, before the depredations of Henry II and Oliver Cromwell's marauding troops? John Field, in his Kingdom, Power, and Glory (London: James & James, 1996/1999, 147), observes that 'So here it stands, this close-packed chaos of beautiful things and worthless vulgar things, after more than a thousand years of tumultuous history. It has somehow resisted the despoiling of two religious revolutions, fire, neglect, vandalism, riots, air raids, Westminster schoolboys, eighteenth century funerals, tomb-rifling, tourists, sea-coal, industrial pollution, traffic. Simply contemplating its miraculous survival nurtures faith.'

"Though today it is ecumenically all things to all people, yet the great Abbey's purpose—Christian witness—remains. The stabilizing and reassuring rhythms of a thousand years remain with us still. Matins at 7:30, Eucharist at 8:00, Evensong at 5:30. Unchanging.

"'Like a great ocean liner built on Thorney Island but never launched, in each age it gathers souls and harbours them,

and bears them silently on, not through space, but through time' (Field, 154).

* * *

"All my life I'd heard of 'Evensong,' and now I was going to experience it. Outside the great Abbey the cacophony—"

"What's that, Mommy?"

"'Cacophony?' Oh, it means so many sounds at once that you can't think. And they are often sounds that grate on your ears and nerves."

Laughing, Beth agreed. "I think that's a good word."

"—the cacophony created by 7 million people forever on the move; inside, the serenity of a church built for the ages. Only those wishing to worship were permitted inside the gates during the services.

"Once inside the Northwest Tower, I just stood there transfixed as I looked up, up, and up at the great Gothic columns and through the iridescent stained-glass windows. The deep-toned bells were ringing, summoning the faithful, the restless, the weary, the despondent, the heartsick, to drop whatever they were doing and seek quietude.

"I softly walked down the main aisle, found a chair between the Quire and the Sacrarium, then looked up and out through the rainbowish North and South Transept windows, and listened to the bells.

"Then we heard it, the Choir of Westminster, solemnly led by beautifully attired vergers, holding aloft the symbolic verges; the choir (composed of both boys and men) singing all the while, accompanied by the great Westminster organ. I shivered. So it must have been in Solomon's Temple—how could one not be reverent in such a setting?

"Our program began with these words:

"'Welcome to this service. You are sharing in a tradition of worship that has been offered since 1065 when the Abbey was founded by St. Edward the Confessor. You are joining people from all over the world. Whatever your faith and belief, especially if you have little or none, we warmly invite you to take part as you can.

"'Much of the service is sung by the choir alone. You worship chiefly by listening, meditating, praying, and letting the music and words take your minds and souls into God's presence. Please join in the hymns and in those parts of the service printed in bold type.'

"The service proceeded, with lessons from Genesis and Romans, followed by Timothy Dudley-Smith's hymn that deeply moved me, perhaps because so many young voices were singing words such as these:

"'Child of the stable's secret birth,
the Lord by right of the lords of earth,
let angels sing of a king new-born
the world's weaving a crown of thorn:
a crown of thorn for that infant head
cradled soft in the manger bed.

"'Eyes that shine in the lantern's ray;
a face so small in its nest of hay,
face of a child who is born to scan
the world of men through the eyes of man;
and from that face in the final day,
earth and heaven shall flee away. . . .

"'Infant hands in a mother's hand
for none but Mary can understand
whose are the hands and the fingers curled

Westminster Abbey Quire

117

but his who fashioned and made our world:
and through these hands in the hour of death
nails shall strike to the wood beneath.'

"After the vergers had led the choir and speakers out, the organist let out his stops and the organ shook the very foundation of the Abbey. When he finished, echoes reverberated against wall after wall and on into infinity.

"Then I got up and studied the rest of the cathedral. Canon N. T. Wright was kind enough to lead me to Poet's Corner, where the likes of Chaucer, Shakespeare, Dickens, Herrick, and Houseman are immortalized.

"Much later I made my way out into the sunset, so overloaded with sensory impressions and undealt-with thoughts that I almost felt I was in a trance."

* * *

"Oh, Mommy, this was the best day yet! He was right in all he said about the Abbey. I—I just wish I had the right words to say what's in my heart. It's so *full!*"

"I know, dear. So is mine."

"But of everything I've ever seen in my life, I think I like Evensong best. . . . Can't tell you why. It's just that it was so-o-o beautiful!"

DAYS NINE-ELEVEN: Canterbury

"Mommy, I'm sad."

"Why, dear?"

"We're coming to the end of these fun trips. He said yesterday was his last day in London."

"Why don't we see what he has for today? Let's see. Oh my!"

"Oh my what?"

"He went to Canterbury!"

"Read it!"

"After a week in London it was time to move on—move on to legendary Canterbury, site of pilgrimages ever since Archbishop Thomas Becket was murdered on December 29, 1170 in the cathedral by minions of Henry II. And certainly Chaucer's Canterbury Tales, Tennyson's Becket, and T. S. Eliot's Murder in the Cathedral have helped to keep Canterbury alive in hearts and minds down through the centuries.

"I took the train so as to really see the countryside. It's only about an hour and a half journey. Immediately upon disembarking you feel you are in a medieval town. In fact, it dates all the way back to the Romans. In 597 Saint Augustine and his fellow missionaries brought Christianity to Britain. Here is where they settled down and built their first church.

"A taxi took me to County Hotel, the cellars of which have been there ever since the twelfth century. Doubtless, Chaucer was familiar with it himself.

"Outside my window, instead of the luminous Tower Bridge, were medieval buildings and streets, townspeople, students from all over the world, and tourists. The bells of the cathedral remind the visitors that it continues to rule the town.

"The poor Cathedral has certainly not had an easy time of it. The sanctuary built by Saint Augustine was sacked and set on fire by the invading Danes in 1011. In 1066 it was wrecked beyond repair by a disastrous fire and had to be rebuilt from the ground up. In 1174 it was ravaged by fire again. In 1377 the old Romanesque nave was demolished in order to construct the great Gothic one. In 1540 Henry VIII's henchmen carried off cartloads of its greatest treasures. But worst of all were the Puritans who, during the 1640s and 1650s toppled the altar and monuments, ripped down the hangings, and badly damaged the organ. Timbers were removed and both ceiling vaulting and roof were stripped. The archives and libraries were plundered. Stained-glass windows were smashed; but fortunately, most survived, for they represent one of the greatest treasures of today's England. Two million visitors a year still come here (compared to Saint Paul's 2.5 million and Westminster's 3 million).

"Since Evensong has got into my blood, when the bells began to ring late in the afternoon I wended my way toward the Cathedral. Inside, the worshipers being rather few that day, they motioned me to sit in the majestic Quire (choir) itself. After the bells, the Canterbury Choir came in, led by the vergers and speakers. Again I was overcome by the synthesis of the visual and the aural"—

"What's 'aural'?"

"What you hear, darling."

"Oh."

"—the radiance of the windows of the Corona, the intricacy of the vaulting, the great columns soaring heavenward, the ancient hand-carved quire, the boys' and mens' voices rising and falling, the speakers' voices, the organ's full-throated vox, and those who participated like me, in order to experience the presence of God once again."

* * *

"I've been to Evensong again, and I've explored the cathedral, top to bottom. Of all the cathedrals in England, this one is unique. What with its ties to Saint Augustine, its being the cradle of English Christianity, its being the mother church of the world-wide Anglican communion, and having its own murder drama—well, it's got it all.

"But I love it for yet another reason. It is quieter here, more serene. The town is relatively small and still medieval, so it's easier here to get lost in a time warp.

"Tomorrow I return to London for my last Evensong."

"Mommy, let's go!"

"Go where, dear?"

"Canterbury! He said it's only an hour and a half away."

"Oh, I don't know. . . ."

"What else do we have to do?"

"Guess you're right, dear. Let's get there in time for Evensong.

* * *

"We did it, Mommy!"

"Yes, dear, we did it—even getting reservations in the County Hotel. I like this town, this cathedral, very much. It is more peaceful than London, and I especially need that peace right now."

"Me, too, Mommy. Especially when Father doesn't want me."

DAY TWELVE: Evensong

"We got our same room again, Mommy?"

"Yes. They promised to hold Room 507 for us. So there's our bridge. It hasn't gone away. . . . It was special in Canterbury, wasn't it? And we saw so much that second day."

"Yep. Loved the whole town."

"Are you ready for the last day's journal entry?"

"No! I don't want it to ever end!"

"I'm afraid it has to. Let's see how he ends it."

"Am back in my old room at the Tower Thistle. And the bridge is still there. This afternoon, one last time, I attended Evensong in Westminster Abbey. It was raining, but inside I felt protected, warmed, and nearer my Creator than I did on sunny days. The Abbey felt more like a refuge.

"As always, I scanned the faces of those who were sharing Evensong with me—searching for her. Who she will be, I don't really know. I only know that I've been praying for her ever since my first Evensong. Asked God to bring her into my life so that I won't be so lonely anymore. And perhaps she's just as lonely as I."

"You are, Mommy, you are!" interjected Beth.

Constance blushed 10 shades of red and reached across to tickle Beth. "You silly girl! Why, I don't even know the man!"

Beth wriggled in delight that she had her mother on the defensive. "Do too. Did you know Father as well when you married him?"

"Well, evidently not, dear. But you're acting a little crazy today."

Beth only looked searchingly at her mother.

"But back to Evensong. My heart is so full this last night in London that I'm just going to let this journal ramble to a close. The very name, Evensong, whispers peace and tranquility. My mind is still seething, still churning, with no closure on this trip. I've been more deeply moved by the Evensongs I've attended than by any other service I can remember. Not just by the service itself, but by the commitment made by the Church of England—that day in, day out, one of the verities of British life is that one can depend on meeting God every morning at Matins, and every evening at Evensong. In most American churches one worships God on Sabbaths (but in truth, many only attend on high days, such as Christmas or Easter).

"Modern life appears to be, more and more, akin to a blitzkrieg, to fire and storm, to an irresistible invading force. All around me every day the world seeks to batter me into its own mold. Everywhere I turn, everywhere I go, even in my own home, the world clutches at me. Computers, the Internet, faxes, e-mails, telephones, pagers, radio, videos, television, cinema, music, newspapers, magazines, books, billboards (studies reveal that the average 20 year old has already been exposed to more than a million commercials!). Taken all together, it's almost impossible to hold out against it.

"But just think—what if we all had the opportunity to escape the world twice a day—or at least at Evensong—and for a few blessed moments seek out God, asking for strength and divine peace? Might we not be a different civilization? What if not just Episcopal churches but churches of all faiths kept their doors open all week long? What if all churches had bells, and they rang them morning and evening, calling anyone who sought strength for the day and the Lord's peace to come in? Might not even Britain's 80 percent who are stressed to the breaking point somehow find peace? Maybe we can't all afford to build great Gothic cathedrals, but surely we could recognize the role that beauty and esthetics play in our sanctuaries. Look at God's blueprints for the glorious tabernacle and Temple in the Old Testament. And too often we blunt the soul with the cheap, the prefab, the just plain ugly, instead of searching for beauty, for the sublime.

"So much for my soap box. Nobody's listening to me anyhow."

Beth's laugh tinkled adorably. "He doesn't even know he's being listened to, does he?"

"No, indeed!" laughed her mother.

"Just what am I looking for in this world of hedonism, secularism, and obsession with pleasure and self-gratification?"

"Big words again, Mommy."

"Yes, dear. 'Hedonism' means to live only for pleasure—not others; 'secularism' means a life without God; and the other words mean the same things."

"Oh."

"I'm looking for a woman who will wear well"—

"Wear *what* well?"

"Oh, you darling little ducky!" laughed her mother. "He means a woman he wouldn't get tired of, even when she gets old."

"No one could ever get tired of *you*, Mommy."

"You and your one-track mind," said her mother, smiling. "But I thank you for the compliment just the same."

"Of course externals are important, but what's inside is even more so. Is she kind, loving, unselfish, empathetic, sweet, giving, honest, altruistic, industrious"—

"Stop, Mommy."

"I knew you'd stop me—you always want to understand every word, bless your heart. 'Empathetic' means you try really hard to see life through other people's eyes so you can understand them, comfort them, and encourage them. 'Altruistic' means you do nice things for people 'just because' instead of expecting them to do nice things back."

Beth wore a thoughtful look, then sighed. "Those are hard to do."

"Does she love beauty wherever it might be found? Does she love children?"

"He must like children a lot!"

"Apparently, dear."

"Will she revel in walks along the beach, hikes in the mountains, getting lost in old bookstores? Will she love both the familiar and the faraway places? Will she cry at sad movies, sad music, sad books?"

"He's talking about *you*, Mommy."

"Hush, you romantic child!"

"Will she consider each day to be an adventure, a gift from God, an opportunity to make a difference in the lives of others? Will she be intelligent and enjoy the deep things of life? Will she have a good sense of humor? (She'd have to, to survive me!)"

"He makes me laugh!" broke in Beth.

"Will she stay with me for life (not just until she finds someone she likes better than me)? Most of all, will she have a deep and abiding faith in God? If she should not, not all these other wonderful qualities could possibly compensate.

"Tomorrow I board the great silver bird for home. I really wonder, though, why I've literally poured my heart out onto these pages, making myself so vulnerable (should anyone else perchance see them). But that's so unlikely that I certainly can rule that out!"

"Wrong again, huh, Mommy?"

Her mother only smiled enigmatically and read on.

"But you, Tower Bridge, out there in the falling rain, do you see me? You know, Bridge, I feel I know you well enough to confide in you. Tell you what: I'd like to come back to this very city this Christmas season. Come back to London to see Dickens' Christmas Carol performed, to see Saint Nicholas ride in on his gray horse, to see all the Christmas decorations.

"Most of all—is this dream truly impossible?—I'd like to

have her with me. I'd like to hold her hand during Evensong and make her blush by whispering to her how lovely I think she is, and how much I love her.

"And sooner or later, I want a little girl that looks just like her.

"Please, dear God?"

There was a long silence, broken finally by Beth's "I'm *so* glad he didn't forget me."

"You darling, darling child!" responded her mother, hugging her.

* * *

"Mommy, you've got to send it back to Mr. Harrison."

"All right. Let's look in every crevice of this thing. . . . Not here. Not here. Not he— Oh! There's something in this pocket. A business card with his Jackson Hole address."

"In Wyoming?"

"Yes."

"Oh, goody! I *love* Wyoming!"

"You, my dear, are impossible. But for *your* sake we'll copy the card and mail the journal back to him."

"With a letter from me in it—and a letter from you. Explaining things?"

"W-e-l-l, I guess that would be polite of us."

"Mommy, sometimes you are the one who's impossible."

POSTLUDE

[In Harrod's department store]. "Look, Mommy! Here's his newest book!"

"Who, my dear?"

"You know very well what who! The only who we've been talking and thinking about. Sometimes I don't know about you, Mommy. . . . Look, here's his picture! Just as I thought he'd look!"

"Oh?"

"Yes. Tall, handsome (but not too much), smile thingies in his cheeks and eyes—and he's looking at me and telling me to just be patient. Don't *you* like him?"

"Why, uh, yes. He looks like a nice man."

Beth did not respond in mere words, but her eyes could have killed.

* * *

It was snowing in the Tetons. William walked over to the window of his great log cabin home, flanked by flocked evergreens, and stared across the valley at a sight he never grew tired of—Mount Moran and the saw-bladed Teton peaks leaping into the sky nearly 8,000 feet from the valley floor. Without question, one of the grandest sights on this planet. So high was his ranch on the east mountainside that he could see both the falling snow and the sunlight glowing on Grand Teton Peak, framed for the moment against an azure sky. Then that vista narrowed as the storm engulfed even the high country.

He returned to his seat by the crackling fire in the towering three-story-high rock fireplace. His thoughts, with a determined will of their own, carried him back to London. Just what had he accomplished there? Was it all a fool's journey? He mused, *I'm still convinced God sent me there—but for what purpose? As far as I know, she was not there. And all that work I put in on my journal—lost!* His last hope had been dashed by a telephone call from the general manager of the Tower Thistle Hotel.

"Sorry, sir, but I had security check your room. No journal anywhere."

Idly, he turned to the large stack of unread mail. It made him tired just to look at it, the work it represented. Especially the book-related fan mail, for it was virtually impossible to keep up with it. But one package was thicker than the rest, and it was hand-addressed. The smoothly-flowing calligraphy was something out of the past, not the computerized present. The stamps, too, were chosen for their beauty. No blah metered postmark here. He opened it.

Unbelievably, *here was his lost journal!* He couldn't believe it! But how—? Perhaps the letters would tell the story. He opened the most interesting looking one first. Never could resist letters from children with their large scrawled or hand-blocked letters on the envelope. So undeveloped spatially that almost invariably they'd run out of space and have to cramp the rest of the letters into a huddle at the end. But this one made it. A girl, he guessed, 7 to 10 years of age, probably. Inside was some crayoned artwork—the Tower Bridge! Remarkably good for a child. Already she had developed a sense of symmetry. He turned to her letter and smiled as he read it.

"Dear Mr. Harrison,

"Thank you for writing your journal. Mommy found it behind the dresser. Please don't be mad at me because I made Mommy snoop. I just couldn't have lived without seeing what was in it!

"We—at least *I*—love it. I don't know about Mommy. She hides how she feels more than I do. We read every word. Weren't we naughty?

"I like you very much. Would you write to me? Or are you too busy to write to a girl who is only 7 years old?

"I have a lot more to say, but Mommy is rushing me. Next time I'll say more. If there is a next time. Oh I DO hope so!

Love

Beth

The other letter was written in that same beautiful script. In it, the girl's mother told him the story of their finding his journal, their decision to read it, their following in his footsteps each day, and their finding his card.

"Let me tell you a little about my precocious little Beth. She's such an intense little darling. She'd been terribly disappointed (upon our arrival in London) when the object of our visit failed to show up. So there we were, with lots of time on our hands, and nothing to do. Your journal gave us an excuse to play tourist and see England from the perspective of an American visitor.

"More significantly, during the reading of it Beth became more and more fascinated with you. I've never before seen her take to a person as she has you. In fact, had it not been for her, this packet would have included no letters, just an explanatory note. She's absolutely set her heart on hearing back from you. It would mean so much to her if you would—even if it were but a short note."

There was more, but it was guarded and rather reserved. He read between the lines and wondered whether or not she was still married. Of course he answered Beth's letter. Both letters. He couldn't help thinking as he did so whether God was at the bottom of all this. In closing he asked both of them if they'd be interested in continuing the correspondence.

They were, so letters began flowing between Santa Fe and Jackson Hole.

* * *

"Got my third letter today," bragged Beth.

"I got one too," admitted her mother.

"He got my picture and likes it! Says he'd like even more the original to it some day," chortled Beth. "Did you send him one of you?"

"No, dear."

"How come?"

"Because, oh, how can I explain? Well, it's because I've already been burned when a certain man didn't look beyond my face and figure. I want—*someday*—to be, uh, appreciated because of what I am inside."

"But how would he know that you're beautiful?"

"Well, I guess that's a chance he'd have to take, dear."

"Have I told you lately that sometimes you're impossible, Mommy?"

"Yes," laughed her mother.

* * *

"Got another letter. Picture, too."

"Good. What did he have to say?"

"Why? Didn't he write you too?"

"Yes," blushed her mother. "Never mind."

* * *

The question that had been gnawing on him the most was answered by Beth. Volunteered, as he hadn't known how to ask it:

"Let me tell you about Mommy and my father. He didn't love her very much, so they divorced. He doesn't love me very much, either. I can understand why he wouldn't love me, but I can't understand why he wouldn't love her! 'Cuz she's the most wonderful woman in all the world! When I tell her how pretty she is, she just smiles and says, 'Darling' (she calls me that a lot!), 'the only beauty that counts comes from inside you.'"

In his sixth letter he asked Constance for her phone number. Thereafter, the friendships took on a new voice-enriched dimension. He would smile to himself when Beth would say, "It's Mommy's turn to talk now."

The telephone topics ranged from news of the day to the Eternal. Constance plied him with questions relating to his faith journey. He listened intently as she updated him on Beth. It almost seemed he'd always been her friend as she shared with him her likes, her hopes, her dreams. Gradually, Constance found herself opening up more and more. Having the letters focused on God and Beth first, then their shared love of books and the arts, helped that. She didn't spare herself.

After a time, when her confidence in him had increased, she openly confessed her wandering from God and the mistakes of her past. Increasingly, she realized that she shared things with William (now Bill) that she'd never told anyone before.

One day the conviction came to her that she could talk so openly with Bill because she *trusted* him. That she should ever again completely trust a man so jolted her that she dropped into a nearby chair to savor the idea. A smile tickled the corners of her mouth, and she gave fervent thanks that Beth, back in school, didn't see her at that moment. Beth would have seen her very soul shining from her face—and would have known the reason. For Beth harbored none of her mother's compunctions and reservations. Her correspondence with Harrison remained as it had been from the first—open, confident, wistful, yearning, as though she had searched for him all her life.

E-mails came next. And he'd call them from various cities where he was doing book signings. His voice on the phone did things to her that Robert's voice never had. Yet she resisted his efforts to get together with her and Beth in person. Why, she really wasn't sure, but she sensed that what they had was such a rare meeting of the inner spirits that to inject the physical dimension prematurely might very well jeopardize *everything*. Knowing how deeply she had been hurt, he—rather gradually, it must be admitted—acceded to her wish.

But in doing so he became party to something rare in contemporary society. In their letters each fell in love with the very soul of the other. The real-life chemistry was a wild card that could be dealt with later. Should that crucial dimension not be there when they finally met, well, they'd remain soul mates anyway. Meanwhile, Constance and Beth's love for God increased and deepened.

He sent her a music box that played only one song— "To Love Again." Beth was fascinated by it and was always winding it up just to hear it again.

One day, as he was looking through his mail, he found a large envelope with the now familiar childish handwriting on it. Smiling, he opened it to see what Beth had to say. Down the page a little were these words:

"Mr. Harrison. Feels funny to still call you that. You mean so much more than that to me. And to Mommy. You make her so happy her eyes dance. She sings all the time. Yet we never really see you. We only imagine you. That's kinda sad. Had my eighth birthday yesterday, and you weren't there. I missed you. I'm growing up without you. Do you want me to grow up without you? Do you really love me as much as I love you? Do you really love Mommy? If you do, *do* something! I cried yesterday when you didn't even call to wish me happy birthday. Then Mommy reminded me I'd never told you when my birthday was. But you should have asked! Now Christmas is coming, and if you don't come for that I shall die."

Nothing in Harrison's life had ever moved him more than this letter. This letter from a girl who was already bridging into adolescence. Did he want her to complete that bridge without him? Did he want her and Constance—she now let him call her Connie—to celebrate Christmas without him? Not on his life!

He reached for the phone and called his travel agent, and ordered three tickets to London.

* * *

It was Christmas in London. The great city had bestirred itself to ready for the season of the Christ Child, and was as festive as one ever sees it.

The great bells of Westminster Abbey were ringing out the news that Christmas Evensong was only minutes away. A beautiful woman stood next to the gate with an almost carbon-copy child beside her. Both wore an air of extreme expectancy, waiting the arrival of a man they had never seen.

Then, around the corner he came at a brisk pace. Seeing them, he slowed, recognizing the little girl by the photo she'd sent him. Ostensibly, he saw only the shy child, standing on one foot, the other nervously digging into the pavement, but in truth he never missed a nuance of the vision standing by her side.

As he reached them he knelt down in front of the child and said, "Merry Christmas, Princess."

She said not a word but solemnly searched his eyes. Meanwhile, her mother missed nothing of the tableau.

Then the little girl bypassed everything that didn't really matter—such as small talk—and rushed to resolution. Her voice shaking because she cared so much about the man's answer, she asked the question she'd been living with night and day for so many long months. "Are you going to be my daddy?"

Just as solemnly he answered, "Would you like me to?"

"Yes. More than anything in all the world!"

As he asked his next question (apparently so lightly, almost, in fact, banteringly), he *knew* that the reality of Connie was greater—*far* greater—than all his dreams. Now that he had finally seen her in person he knew he could never leave London without her. Not another day of her life did he want to miss!

"What about her?" He looked up and held the gaze of the woman named Constance. "Does *she* come with the package?"

"I—I don't know," slowly answered the little girl, struggling against tears. "Sometimes I just don't know what to do with her."

A roguish look came into the woman's eyes, and the wisp of a smile. She looked down at the still-kneeling man and asked a question of her own, a slight tremor in her voice. "Are you sure you want me in the package, too?"

Before answering he again looked at Beth and was engulfed by a tidal wave of love for this child who was almost singlehandedly responsible for this moment of decision. Neither could he even consider leaving London without her! Here was the daughter of his dreams—only he'd already missed more than seven years of her life. He'd not miss another day!

Gathering the still trembling little girl in his arms, he tenderly kissed the tears in her eyes and stood up. Then he turned to the woman and said, "Beth and I have a question." Even without knowing for sure what he would say, Beth kissed his cheek softly and ran her starved fingers through his hair. "Our question is this," he continued. "Will you marry us, to have and to hold, from this day forth, in sickness and in health, as long as we live, so help you God?"

Now it was the woman's turn to puddle up, smiling at them both through brimming eyes, with so much love and trust in her eyes that the man knew the answer had already been given, regardless of what mere words might say. "I'll give you my answer after Evensong" was her answer in words.

"You're silly, Mommy," Beth broke in, "and a terrible tease."

Turning to the man who held her in his arms, she said "Daddy"—and her voice shook as for the first time in her life she called a man that precious word—"will you hold me all during Evensong and whisper that you love me? . . . Oh, Daddy!" Words failing her, she could only convulsively cling to him and weep in relief that the long journey of two was over and the journey of three was about to begin.

Speech failing him, he could only answer by tightening his arms around her. The mother drank in every drop of the moving scene. Whatever remaining reservations she might have had were swept aside by her daughter's yearning question, the man's response, and by the sight of her daughter in Bill's arms. How her heart sang that he had gone to Beth first!

But to keep up appearances, she tried (unsuccessfully, it's true) to be severe by asking him, "And what do you have left for *me?*"

The newly-minted daddy mistily smiled at her, but his voice yet teased. "Well, Beth has taken possession of everything but my right arm. If it promises to hold you close to me, will that do?"

"For the moment," she answered demurely. But her twinkling eyes held both promise and a great love the man recognized for what it was—the answer to his heart-felt prayers.

And so a little girl called Beth, a woman Beth called "Mommy," and a man Beth called "Daddy"—a sacred circle of three—walked into Christmas Evensong.

* * *

How This Story Came to Be

I worked on ideas for this story for six months before the subject finally jelled. In fact, my first story plot sputtered out completely, as dead as Marley's proverbial doornail. The catalyst turned out to be a research trip my wife Connie and I took to London and Canterbury in early January 2001. It was our first trip to England.

The book deadline was upon me, and I still had no twelfth story. Having come to the end of my rope, I turned the story over to God, requesting an additional favor from Him: not only provide me with a Christmas story plot, but make it *an extra special one.*

In late February God answered my supplications. *Take your trip to England and construct a plot upon places where you stay and visit, things you do, and people you meet there. Limit the characters to three—a man, a woman, and a little girl.*

My dilemma was this: How was I to construct a believable romance from a plotline in which the three protagonists never actually see each other until the final scene? I'd never faced a challenge quite like this one in all my years of writing.

I finally concluded that it could be done through the vehicle of a journal (a time-honored literary device). But it wouldn't work if the journal were the typical sequence of private thoughts and observations. Readers of such entries would generally consider them to be self-serving, because all of us see ourselves through rose-tinted glasses. Perhaps a travel-related journal would work. . . . It could be read on many levels, and through its pages the personal revelations could be Trojan-horsed.

My primary objective was to have the woman become so fascinated by the man who wrote the journal entries that she'd be open to love. What I hadn't counted on was Beth, who I initially consider to be almost a cameo character but who ended up running away with the story. Beth falls in love with William long before her mother does. Her father-hunger turns out to be even more intense than her mother's yearning for a soul mate. In fact, were it not for Beth, it's doubtful that a romance between the adult protagonists would have ever developed!

In truth, the story ended up being more about father-hunger than anything else. Since I prayed so continuously for divine guidance as I wrote, I cannot escape the conviction that God willed this unexpected shift of emphasis. We are being sold a bill of goods today: that fathers are optional; that a woman can do very well in raising a child without a husband. While this may be true for a woman, we are belatedly discovering it most definitely is *not* true for a child.

In marriage 99 percent of the way we act as a spouse or a parent is determined by the example-prototypes we observed in our parents. Realizing this, it should come as no surprise that girls who grow up without a father figure have no idealized prototype on which to base either a choice of a husband or knowledge of how to jointly raise a child. Boys, if anything, are worse off, because they face huge difficulties in learning what it means to be a man, a husband, or a father.

My heart goes out to all those children who are so starved for not just a father, but a *daddy* in their lives. These children who daily experience the void that only a daddy can fill instinctively know that they are being shortchanged.

With all these variables in mind, let's return to little Beth. In the pages of this journal she gradually discovers that a potential father could be a pied piper who leads her into magical worlds she has never known much about. Worlds of the mind, the humanities—history, geography, literature, architecture, art, music, religion. Instinctively, she senses that it is this man's relationship with God that sets him apart from other men she has closely observed.

In these pages she learns to trust him—the ultimate tribute a child can give to an adult. Knowing her mother as she does (typical of mother/daughter households), without realizing that she's reversing roles, she precipitates the action that forces her mother to seriously consider marriage with this man they know only through journal pages. If he could be brought to the point where he falls in love with her adorable mother and would promise before God to marry her and stay with her "until death do us part," if he could be a really truly daddy who loves her as much as her mother does, then the three of them would indeed become a divinely ordained circle of three—a family.